TEMBA DAWN

TEMBA DAWN

Alec Lea

CHARLES SCRIBNER'S SONS
NEW YORK

Dedicated
to My Mother

1 3 5 7 9 11 13 15 17 19 V/C 20 18 16 14 12 10 8 6 4 2
Manufactured in the United States of America
Library of Congress Catalog Card Number 75-4346
ISBN 0-684-14386-0

Contents

I

The Birthday Present

Rob was looking forward to his tenth birthday so much
that he could think of nothing else. He was going to be
ten on the 25th of September and all through that
month the first thing he did when he came home from
school was to go and look at his birthday present. It
was always there, in the second of the big cow-byres at
Tomallen Farm where he had lived all his life. It was
always there because the cows were always brought in
for milking at half past four and his birthday present
always came in with them.

He had just made a new friend at school, a town boy
called David who didn't know anything about farms
but wanted to know a lot. On the 18th of September,
just a week before his birthday, he invited David to go
home with him to the farm to see his present.

On the way home Rob tried to explain the situation,
which he knew would seem complicated to anyone who
didn't know about farming.

'Of course, you won't actually be able to *see* my
present,' he said. 'You'll only be able to see the big
black bulge where it lives.'

David stared at Rob. 'Bulge? What the heck d'you
mean? Is it all wrapped up or something?'

'Yes, it certainly *is* wrapped up,' said Rob. 'So
wrapped up that no one's seen it yet, no one at all in the

whole world.'

'You said your dad was giving it to you,' said David, beginning to feel that Rob must be pulling his leg.

'So he is, but he hasn't *seen* it, at least only the bulge part of it.'

By this time the two boys were entering one of the two big cow-byres at Tomallen Farm. John the cowman was busy milking; the electric motor that worked the milking machines was purring away in the enginehouse and the steady tick-tock of the pulsators squeezing the milk out of the cows' teats could be heard all through the byre. David had never seen cows being milked before and was rather impressed. There were about twenty huge black-and-white Friesian cows in that byre, all standing very quietly either eating cowcake or chewing the cud.

Rob led David down to one end and stopped him behind a very big cow called Tarbo. She had a shining coat and a very long thin tail with a big bushy tassel at the end, which had evidently just been washed. She was mostly black except for her underparts and her udder which were all white and clean. Her name was written on a slate fixed to the wall above her head. Every cow had her own slate, with other details written on it besides her name.

'Look,' said Rob, 'that's Tarbo and it says on her slate that she's dry and is going to calve on the 25th. That's my birthday and that's where my present is, see?'

He pointed to one of Tarbo's great bulging flanks, the one on the right side.

8

David was looking at everything with great interest, but there was so much to look at and it was all so new and strange to him that he wasn't very quick in the uptake.

'D'you mean *that's* your present, that whoppin' great cow?' he asked in horror.

'No, you twit, not her—what's inside her. Look, come here.'

Rob made David come right behind the cow so that he could see that she had a much bigger bulge on her right side than on her left. Then he stepped up into her stall on the right and spread the palm of his hand on the bulgiest part of the bulge.

'Now, watch!' he said to David.

Rob pushed his hand with all his strength against the bulge, repeated the pressure two or three times, then took his hand away. Both boys watched intently, in silence. At first nothing happened except that Tarbo swung her head round and took a long calm look at them with very dreamy and friendly eyes. Then something moved inside the bulge, something obviously alive and pushing to get out. It was rather like what happens when you disturb a cat that's gone to sleep under a thick eiderdown on a bed—the eiderdown suddenly swells up in one place and gives you a shock.

David looked frightened but Rob laughed.

'There,' he said, 'now you've seen my present at last. That's her calf and as soon as it comes out it'll be mine.'

David was looking at Tarbo very hard. 'But how's it ever going to *get* out?' He couldn't see any opening in the cow's body that would be big enough to let out a

9

calf.

'Oh well, she has to push like anything *here*,' Rob replied, holding her tail aside and pointing to her back parts.

'Have you ever seen a calf come out?' asked David.

'Of course, I know all about those things,' said Rob quickly. But the next moment he wished he had not said that, because he could guess from David's eyes that he suspected it wasn't true. There must have been a false note in Rob's voice. As a matter of fact, he never had actually seen a calf being born, he had always got there either just too late or just too early. That was not surprising, because although it usually takes a cow three or four hours of hard work to get ready for the final push, that final push itself very often only takes two or three minutes. And it is only the final push, when the calf at last comes right out into the cold and starts to breathe for itself, that is really thrilling to watch. All the rest is rather boring and needs an awful lot of patience, usually in the dark and the cold, for cows seem to prefer to calve in the quiet hours of the night or very early in the morning.

Rob decided then and there that he would make a very special effort to see *this* calf being born. 'Anyway,' he said, 'I'm definitely going to be there when this one comes out. P'rhaps I'll even be able to help Tarbo with it.'

'Oh, you *lucky* thing!' said David, green with envy. 'I wish *I* could. Couldn't you let me—send me a message—'

Rob told him sadly that he didn't see how it would be

possible. 'Not unless you were staying here,' he said. 'You see, even if she started calving in daytime at the weekend, and I telephoned you, you'd have to come all the way from Bridge of Don. Would you be allowed to come out on your bike?'

'Not alone, no,' said David.

'You see,' Rob went on, 'I shall probably have to get up in the middle of the night and go out in the fields. I shall have to borrow Dad's special torch. 'Course he might come with me. Our cows calve out in the fields till it's nearly winter.'

'Will it be a he or a she calf?' David asked.

'I want it to be a heifer, of course,' Rob replied, trying not to smile. 'Because then I'll be able to keep her for years, ten years perhaps. But no one can tell. If it's a bull then he'll have to be castrated and will only live about two years. But Dad says there's lots of hope it'll be a heifer because Tarbo's last two have been bulls.'

When the two boys went in for tea Rob asked his father, 'Dad, have you seen Tarbo today?'

'Yes, son, I had a good look at her this morning. She's going to be well on time.'

'You mean she'll calve on my birthday?'

'I've told you several times I can't promise that. But I'm sure it'll be a near thing, twenty-fourth, fifth or sixth I would say.'

'Dad, will you be able to tell a bit better next week— I mean, isn't there *something* that tells you that it's coming next day or p'rhaps in a few hours?'

'Well, all right, I'll tell you the secret,' said his father thoughtfully, noticing how very anxious his son was about his calf. 'Unless a cow gets badly upset or frightened, she'll never calve until she's got a full bag of milk for her calf. So you must keep looking at a cow's udder, keep watching it and feeling it every day for the last fortnight before she calves. Then if her udder suddenly fills right up and feels properly tight, and if you try the teats and milk comes spurting out under pressure, then you can bet your bottom dollar she'll calve in six to twelve hours.'

The two boys recognised the voice of the expert, so as soon as tea was over they ran back to the byre to make a special examination of Tarbo's udder. But it was too late, the cows had all gone back into the fields.

2
The Birth of Temba Dawn

The next afternoon Rob went to the byre alone, taking a tape-measure with him. John the cowman was just putting the machine on the cow next to Tarbo, so Rob was able to get his opinion on when her calf would be born.

About a week yet, John reckoned. He said she was shaping well and was going to have a lot of milk. 'One of our best milkers, she is. Ought to do six gallons a day and keep it up through the winter.'

Then John watched with curiosity while Rob put the tape-measure round Tarbo's udder for the second time and took another reading. 'What's the idea o' that?' John asked.

'So's I can tell how it grows. Dad says it may get big suddenly and then she'll calve quick—but supposing I didn't notice?'

'Smart laddie then,' said John with a big laugh. 'But I'm the one to tell ye when she's ready. I've been watching her every day for a month, so I should ken.'

Five afternoons later, on the 24th, John was not there in the byres because it was his Sunday half holiday, so Rob's father was doing the milking.

Rob measured Tarbo's udder and then rushed over to the other byre where his father was handling the machines.

'Dad, her udder's gone up three inches since yesterday. Come and see, quick!'

His father looked round at him with a smile. 'What's
the hurry? Do you think it will go down again before I
get there? I noticed when she came in that she was
looking different. She came in last, too.'

Rob hopped about in a state of excitement, helping
his father with the milking machines, but hindering
almost as much. At last they were ready to go into the
other byre and his father came over to give Tarbo a
thorough examination.

He looked at her hips and lifted her tail to see how
the opening underneath was beginning to widen. Then
he patted and smoothed her udder in several places,
finally giving each of her teats a gentle squeeze. Milk
came spurting out of all four of them and continued to
flow after he stopped squeezing, so there was soon a
little pool of milk on the floor.

'Well, that's it, Rob,' he said. 'You're going to be
lucky. She's sure to calve before tomorrow morning.
Now run along to the dairy and do that job I showed
you. I have to go out tonight and I'm in a hurry.'

That it was Sunday evening was another bit of luck
for Rob. Since he had got up late that morning there
was a good chance he would be allowed to stay up later
than usual tonight. He did not ask his father if he could
go out to the fields in the middle of the night, because
he knew he would probably say no. But later on, at tea,
he did ask him if *he* intended to go out in the night.

'I don't reckon there'll be any need,' his father said.
'I've put Tarbo in the nursery field behind the barns,

with those three heifers, so I can have a look at her last thing before going to bed. She's in fine condition, she shouldn't need any help.'

After dark that night, about half past nine, Rob's mother allowed him to go out with a torch to have a last look at Tarbo. His mother knew how excited he was and that he would not sleep until he had seen her again.

He had his father's big powerful torch with him, but there was still a faint after-glow in the western sky and the street lights of Aberdeen were showing up brightly in the south. So he hardly used the torch until he reached the gate which he had to climb over. On the other side of it he sent the torchrays streaming right across the little field and discovered Tarbo at once. She was lying down by herself close to the wall of the big yard, while the three heifers were still grazing over on the other side.

He went up close to her for a good look. She was not chewing the cud, her eyes were no longer at all dreamy, they were rather staring and anxious and she was flopping her tail about on the grass as cows do when they are annoyed about something. Her eyes fixed themselves directly on him and his torch, so much so that he began to feel scared. When she gathered herself together as if to rise, he took two or three quick steps back away from her, so as to be ready to run.

But he stayed all the same and watched her get up on her legs, slowly and heavily, not really wanting to. He felt guilty over that. He was being a nuisance to her. Then she stretched her head and neck round sideways as far as she could and gave herself a few hefty licks on her thigh. As she did so she made a very deep moo, so deep and rumbling that it sounded rather like thunder in the far distance.

Now that she was standing Rob could see that her back parts were different. Her hips were farther apart and the opening under her tail was stretched much wider.

He stayed there watching her for a long while until he began to get cold and there was no light at all in the sky except the electric lights of Aberdeen. Then at last he decided that he would have to go, but he made up his mind at the same time that he would come out again before daylight. He felt sure that he would be able to slip out of the house without making the slightest sound. It seemed a lucky thing that his father had gone into town tonight, because it would mean that he would go to bed late and sleep all the sounder. But before going to bed he would be coming out here to look at Tarbo, Rob suddenly realised. And he would need this big torch. Wouldn't it be awful if Tarbo got started on the job of pushing the calf out just as his father reached the field! Then his father would stay and see everything and in the morning would say to Rob, 'Hard luck, son, it's all over and I'm afraid you've missed it again.' Oh no, he simply wouldn't be able to bear that. He *must* come out again in a few hours' time, well before day-light. But how was he going to wake up, that was the main difficulty. It was so easy for grown-ups. They only had to set their alarm clocks.

It was just after ten o'clock when he finally got into

bed and his mother said goodnight and departed downstairs. He stayed awake listening until his father came in after what seemed about an hour, then he dozed off and must have had a good long sleep, for when he next woke up his window, which he had left uncurtained, showed a glimpse of daylight. He hopped out of bed in a panic and found his watch, which had the sort of face you can see in the dark. It said just after five. The house was absolutely silent, but as he listened he heard a cock crow on the other side of the big yard. Going close to the window he saw there was a long bar of faint daylight in the direction of the sea.

He dressed furiously fast by the light of the little torch he kept under his pillow for emergencies. If he switched on the light it would make a loud click and would show under his door. He put on some thick warm clothes and crept downstairs, still using his little torch. In the passage he picked up his thickest winter anorak, then went through the kitchen and scullery and drew the bolt on the back door without making a sound.

As he softly closed the back door behind him and turned round, he was in another world, a world totally different from the one he had just left. He had crept out of a world of close silence, of beds and sleep and parents and safety, and now here he was in a world of—stars. Yes, stars were the first things he saw, enormously far away in a perfectly clear sky. So it was a fine morning and was most likely going to be a lovely day. But there was a nip of frost in the air.

He knew the sun would rise at about a quarter to

seven, so there ought to be a fair amount of daylight by a quarter past five. It was getting on for that now. And then at about six John would be setting out to bring the cows in. He would most likely come and have a look in the nursery field, too, before going for the cows. So Rob only had about three quarters of an hour, if he wanted to have Tarbo all to himself.

He had to go round behind all the big barns to reach the nursery. Except for cocks crowing from the hen runs, there wasn't a sound of anything moving in the buildings, though he knew that the bull and several young calves were indoors. When he came round on the seaward side of the steading he found there was already more daylight than he had expected. There was such a great orange-coloured glare over the sea that he knew he had been right not to bring his father's heavy torch out again. It was more fun without one and there was light enough to see that there was white frost on the grass in all the places where it had been eaten down bare.

He had never before had the whole farm to himself like this. And it was not only the whole farm, it seemed like the whole world because there were no human sounds to be heard anywhere and the lights of the city were now quite hidden by the barns.

Climbing the gate into the nursery, the first thing he noticed was that she was not in the place close to the yard wall where he had said goodbye to her last night. He went over there first and saw signs that she must have spent some long restless hours there, for the grass was badly trampled and churned up with mud and dung. The next thing he saw was the three heifers lying down all together in the middle of the field. Tarbo was not visible at the moment, but there was a clump of bushes over on the other side, near the drinking trough, which might be hiding her.

As he walked across, not too near the heifers because he didn't want to rouse them, he heard a curlew call very close, then it gave him a fright by flying just over his head, near enough for him to feel the rush of air from its wings. He caught a glimpse of its long curved beak and was glad it had not used it to take a nip at one of his ears. They were being nipped quite enough by the frost.

If he had been older and more experienced in farming matters he would have been able to tell by now that she had not calved yet, or else that she had forced her way through the fence into some other field. For if she had already calved those three heifers would not be lying there asleep in the middle of the field, they would be standing round watching and envying her with her calf. Nothing interests and excites heifers quite so much as a new baby. They always seem to know even when one arrives on the farm next door.

Sure enough Tarbo was there behind the bushes, lying down. When he reached her she was looking round at him, but she made no move to rise. Her eyes were even wider and more alert than they had been last night.

Cautiously, he went up close to see what was happening at her rear end. It was very interesting. A sausage-shaped balloon of stuff like cellophane was sticking out of her and inside it were the ends of two calf's legs, their little black hooves very shiny and plainly recognisable.

Rob was both delighted and rather scared by this sight. Because he had heard his father talk of it, he knew this must be the water-bag which came out just before the final push and which had to burst before the calf could be born. So it looked as if his good luck were holding. For a few minutes now there was nothing to do but wait and watch, so he had time to remember that this was his birthday morning. Fancy forgetting that! He had been awake for a good half hour by this time and it was nearly broad daylight, yet this was the first time he remembered that it was his birthday. Certainly that had never happened before. What was there about this great black Tarbo that was so fascinating that it had made him forget everything else in the world? It was a difficult question. Was it just because she was bringing a brand-new thing into the world (no, not thing, but creature) and that this brand-new creature was going to belong to *him* and him only? Yes, maybe that was it. For this calf would not be Tarbo's for more than an hour or two. His father always liked to take new-born calves away from their mothers at once, because otherwise the mothers always got so fond of their babies that it was cruelty to take them away at all.

But this calf, just as soon as it was taken away from Tarbo, would be *his*. *He* would have to look after it, *he* would have to give it a name—but—yes, a name—and the sort of name it ought to have depended on what sort of calf it was, bull or heifer. So he took a good look at those feet again, inside their cellophane bag, and asked himself very anxiously did they look like male or female feet?

Tarbo was beginning to get to work again. She mooed deeply, stretched her long neck and head out along the ground for a minute, as if she were drawing up strength out of the earth, and then gave a great heaving push. The cellophane bag burst, a gallon of water splashed over the ground, the calf's legs came farther out and were followed by its nose. And then its whole head was suddenly there, steaming, its eyes opening and shutting, its mouth gasping for breath.

Rob could only stand there, staring and wondering.

Tarbo had a few moments' rest after that, before giving the final push. When that came, it was such a strong one that the whole calf slithered far out, leaving a couple of feet of space between mother and child. The calf lifted its head and spluttered, blowing bubbles out of its nose. It was still joined to Tarbo by its navel cord.

Rob was just summoning up enough courage to go nearer and lift the calf's tail (because it's only by looking under the tail that you can tell which sex a new-born calf is), when Tarbo without warning scrambled to her feet, making him step back quickly out of her way. The navel cord broke as she turned round to muzzle her baby.

So Rob had lost his chance. He was pretty sure Tarbo wouldn't mind, but all the same he knew better than to touch any big animal's new baby while its mother was still busy discovering it for the first time.

3
Naming the Calf

When Rob turned away, knowing that he would have to go home now and tell his father, he found that the three heifers had come up close and were lined up watching the calf. They must have been there several minutes, but he had been so taken up with the birth that he had neither seen nor heard them.

He had time now to notice what a splendid morning it was. The sun was going to come up out of the sea into a perfectly clear sky, which already had a blaze of pure gold in it. The air was frosty and biting, but there was not a breath of wind and somehow you knew that summer would be back again by midday. A robin was singing loudly in the bushes and a flock of seagulls went over, heading inland. Usually he was fast asleep in bed at this magic hour. For the first time he wondered if there might be something a little silly about that.

On his way back to the house he heard in the distance John's voice rousing up the cows in a big field on the other side of the steading. So he quickened his pace, for he wanted to be the first to give his father the news.

When he reached the house he saw through the kitchen window that his father was there, having his morning cup of tea. So he entered with a rather scared face, but his father was smiling and seemed to know all about what he had been doing.

'Hullo, birthday boy! So it's born then?'

'*Yes*, Dad, you bet it is, and I saw everything! She's licking it now. And she's ter-*rifi*-cally pleased!'

'Yes, they always are. And you've had quite an adventure, haven't you? Don't take that anorak off, we're going out again in a minute. I must get that calf in at once, before it starts sucking milk. Is it a big one?'

'Oo, yes. An' it's all wet—absolutely soppin' wet and slobbery.'

'So would you be if you'd been in a hot bath for nine months. Well, we'll go and fetch it with a wheelbarrow, I'm not pulling my arms out of their sockets for nothing. You'd better have a drink of milk.'

Soon they were on their way out again, his father taking a barrow and a couple of sacks as they went through the yards. John must have caught sight of them, for they saw him on the top of a wall waving to them, since it was too far for shouting. If he had seen the wheelbarrow he would know what they were about.

The calf was already on its legs when they reached it, with Tarbo making a great fuss over it, licking it as if its life depended on it, but yet stopping every now and then to make silly high-pitched little heifer-moos, very different from her deep ones before it was born.

Rob's father supported the calf with one hand, since its legs were nearly folding up all the time, and with the other lifted its tail for Rob to see underneath.

'Which is it, son?'

'Heifer!' cried Rob in delight, exploring the calf's rear end with his fingers to make sure. Yes, besides the little round anal opening, high up under the tail, that all calves would have, it had another lower down, a vertical slit about one inch long.

'Seems to me, Rob, you're just about the luckiest laddie in all Scotland today.'

The farmer wrapped one of the sacks round the calf, sank nearly to his knees and then, using all his strength, lifted it off the ground and laid it on its side in the barrow, with the other sack beneath it. It struggled and nearly fell out, but he seized it again just in time and pressed it down. Then he grasped the barrow's handles and started off at a good pace across the paddock, telling Rob to walk beside it and stop it from getting on to its feet. It was a difficult, awkward business, especially as Tarbo came along too, very close behind, getting excited and anxious.

They were soon at the gate, where the farmer had to stop for a rest because it was such hard work. Mopping his brow, he said, 'Open the gate, Rob, but shut it behind us because of those heifers.'

'What about Tarbo?'

'She'll have to come with us. If we leave her here without her calf she'll be away over the fence in no time at all. She'll not calm down till she's been milked and put back with the cows.'

The heifers tried to come too, but Rob just managed to get the gate closed in their faces.

His father stopped again in one of the outer yards.

'Listen,' he said, 'it sounds as if John's bringing the cows into the byres. If they see or smell this new calf they'll get wild and he'll have a job tying them up.'

So they waited round the corner out of sight while

they could hear the byres filling up and while Tarbo stood close to the barrow licking her calf.

'Poor Tarbo,' said the farmer, talking to her and Rob at the same time and rubbing one hand up and down her massive neck, 'I'm afraid you're going to lose that baby now and you may never clap eyes on it again till it's nearly as big as you. But you'll soon forget if we give you some of our very best hay. I bet you've got a mighty thirst on you, too.'

Rob looked at Tarbo very sadly. 'Will she really forget, Dad?'

'Och yes, just as soon as she's back with all her friends. Cows are very sociable creatures, you know—they all have their special buddies and they hate to be separated from the herd.'

Then they continued their way round the corner into the inner yard and so into the first byre where Tarbo belonged. She by force of habit walked straight along into her usual stall, where she started drinking from her water-bowl even before she was tied up. But the farmer wheeled her calf away in the other direction into a loose-box and dumped it out on to a nice bed of clean straw. John came along, took one good look at it and said,

'So it's a heifer, eh?'

'How did you know?' asked Rob.

'Och weel, I can tell 'em by the shape o' their heads.'

Rob's father told him he could have his calf to himself now and that he ought to make a start with teaching it how to drink.

'But what do I *do*, Dad?'

25

'Just give it a finger to suck. Maybe it *will* suck, maybe it won't. But if it will, that'll mean it's ready for milk and I'll be back again in a wee while with some of Tarbo's as soon as I've milked her out.'

The calf was lying down, tired after its struggles to stand up in the barrow. Rob kept on trying with his finger, but at first it wasn't interested and he was afraid of getting bitten. Several times he managed to get the finger properly in, so that he could feel its sharp teeth, and since he didn't know, or had forgotten, that cattle can't bite because they only have front teeth in the lower jaw, he was naturally a bit nervous.

But this finger-in-mouth business didn't seem to make much sense. The calf obviously thought it a proper nuisance. So Rob gave up for a while and started what seemed the more important job of thinking up a name for it.

He remembered one heifer calf about a year ago that had been named Holy Frieda because it had been born on Good Friday. Could he get a clue from that? Was it possible to make a name out of September? No, it was too long, and also too dull. His calf had been born early in the morning, early on a September morn. In the dawn, in fact. In a September dawn. September Dawn sounded good, but rather too long. Why not Tember Dawn, then? Yes—but why not Temba with an a, because lots of girls' names ended with an a, didn't they?

Suddenly he knew he had a name now, a new one, a real one, a name with a flourish to it. Temba Dawn. Yes, indeed. That was what his calf was going to be called.

He tried it on his tongue. He put a hand under the calf's chin, lifted its head and said to it, right into its big and frightened eyes, 'Hullo, Temba Dawn! I hope you're going to have a nice happy life. And a long one too.'

He had to start thinking then about this calf's childhood, which might last two years, or perhaps two and a half, that was about all, because he knew that heifers were put to the bull at about one year and a half and then had babies nine months later. So in two years' time, when he would still be only twelve years old, hardly yet starting secondary school, Temba Dawn would be almost grown-up. What an awful long time it took for human children to get grown-up!

Well then, he thought, what would it really be like to be a calf instead of a boy? He decided that he wouldn't really mind being one, especially if he could have a Rob to look after him, for this Rob was quite a good chap, a reliable sort of chap.

'Well then,' he said out loud to Temba Dawn, 'I'm going to look after you like anything, I'm going to make sure you *do* have a happy time over your life.'

Only the trouble was, he suddenly realised, that *he* was going to be only twelve, or thirteen, or fourteen, or fifteen, during nearly all of Temba Dawn's life, and teenage boys couldn't really pull very much weight in the world yet, could they?

After all that amount of thinking, what a relief it was to get back to the straightforward job of getting his finger into her mouth. And now, although only five minutes had gone by, things were different. His finger could stay inside, the warm wet mouth started to welcome it, to begin to try swallowing it and then at last to suck. It was a very feeble lazy sucking at first, but gradually it grew stronger and stronger and then suddenly she was on her feet sucking like mad, sucking as if her life depended on it. And as a matter of fact her life did depend on it.

Rob was very pleased that his father came back at just that moment and saw the calf really going for his finger with all her strength.

'Good,' said the farmer, 'that'll save a bit of time. Here, Rob, put your hand in this bucket and let her have a go at that finger under the milk.'

The farmer held the calf between his knees to keep her on her legs, then brought the bucket up until her nose dipped into it. Rob had to try several times to get his finger into her mouth in the new under-milk position, but he managed it in the end and then the sucking got into top gear. While the milk sank down in the bucket Rob grinned widely at his father, who grinned back.

'Good calf,' his father said. 'Very good calf. It's a rare thing for one of 'em to suck as well as this so soon after birth. It's because she never sucked her mother— if she had it might take us two days to get her going as well as this.'

But they were at it nearly a quarter of an hour, for it didn't turn out to be as easy as it looked at first. Several times the calf lost the finger, once or twice she lost her legs, two or three times she lost her temper. She splashed

28

milk over both father and son.

'There, she's had a good half gallon,' said the farmer at last, straightening his back with a sigh of relief. 'That's as much as is good for her the first time. Now leave her alone and she'll sleep for twelve hours.'

4

The Nervous Type

During that Monday Rob was so sleepy in school that
he could hardly keep his eyes open. So he learned nothing. But he had told all his friends that he had got up at
dawn to see the birth and two of them mentioned it to
the teacher when she found him asleep, so she couldn't
get annoyed. Besides, she knew it was his birthday.

David and another friend called Ian went home with
Rob after school for his birthday tea. Of course he took
them first to see Temba Dawn, but on the way he
warned them that if she were still asleep it might be
best not to wake her.

He himself was very impatient to see her again, for
when the other boys had asked him what colour she was
he had said 'mostly black and a little white'; but suddenly he realised now that in fact he hadn't noticed
which parts of her were white. That was silly of him,
because it meant that if she got mixed up with other
calves he would have nothing to recognise her by. There
was another loose-box not far away with three young
calves in it, one of them only ten days old. He had taken
milk to them several times and all of them looked very
much like Temba. They all drank, of course. You only
had to hold a bucket for them and they drained it in
about a quarter of a minute. They were always fright-
fully noisy. He heard them bawling for their evening

milk as soon as he led his two friends into the steading.

'Is yours one o' them makin' that awful racket?' David asked and Rob found he couldn't answer because he didn't know Temba Dawn's voice. There seemed to be a lot that he didn't know about her. Had she even *had* a voice at all, that morning? He thought not.

They were outside her loose-box now, with the door shut and not a sound coming through, not even a rustle of straw. He had the scaring thought that she might have been taken away or had got suddenly ill.

'Sh-sh-sh,' he said, 'she's maybe sleepin'. Wait while I open the door very quietly.'

He pushed at it carefully until he could put his head in. She *was* there, curled up in one corner half buried in straw. 'Okay,' he whispered, pushing the door open a bit more, 'you can come in behind me, only be *quiet.*'

But three pairs of feet made the straw rustle crisply. When they all got close enough for a good view, the calf's eyes opened in a sudden flare of panic, she scrambled to her feet and charged across to the other side of the box, at the same time letting out a piercing bleat of terror. The boys were all too scared to move or speak for a moment, she had taken them so much by surprise.

Rob was the first to shake off his fear. 'I never thought—she'd do *that*!' His voice was a bit unsteady. 'But it's all right, she's just scared stiff of *us*.'

He went up to her very gingerly, stretching out a hand, slowly, to see if he could touch her. She was standing close against the wall, shivering all over. But she let his hand stroke her head and then her back and they could all see how the fear was steadily draining out

31

of her. She was like a child waking out of a nightmare but recovering easily and forgetting it at once.

All the same the noise she had made remained in their ears. It was so full of sheer panic. John must have heard it and taken note of it, for he stuck his head round the door a minute later and sized up the situation with a grin.

'Devil of a scraich it gave! It'll be one of the nervous ones, nae doot. Some are like that, a bit daft-like, but they make fine milkers. I'll be along to feed it in a wee while.'

The boys gathered round Temba Dawn then, to make a pet of her, soon winning her confidence, each of them in turn giving her a finger to suck.

Rob had time now to take proper notice of her markings. She had a white patch on her forehead, a broad scarf of white over one shoulder and white socks on her hind legs. But she had less white than most Friesians. She was a really dark one. Her coat was sleek and shiny now that she was dry.

They had to stay, of course, until John came along with her milk, but then they had a disappointment. He wouldn't leave the bucket with them and let them do the whole job, as Rob asked him to do.

'Look at your clothes,' he said. 'Ye'll be away to your tea in a minute and d'ye want to go in the house soaked wi' milk? I've got kids o' my ain and *I* winna let 'em spoil good clothes.'

They were wearing their school blazers, so Rob had to admit that he was right. But he wouldn't even let them help, he did the whole job himself in very expert style. Temba Dawn behaved a lot better than she had in the morning. In five minutes the milk was all inside her.

'Can I feed her tomorrow?' Rob asked as John was hurrying away back to his cows.

'Ask your dad,' was the reply.

'Let's go and see Tarbo now,' Rob said.

She was quietly munching hay. Her hinder parts still looked different from the other cows, but she seemed to be thinking the same thoughts as they were . . . about food, mainly. Her udder was huge, but she had been milked, John told them.

She had given three gallons.

'What are you going to do with it?' Rob asked, not because he couldn't guess, but because he wanted to impress David and Ian. Ian too was a town boy.

'What her calf doesn't want the pigs'll be glad of— or maybe I'll share it out amongst the other calves.'

'You see,' Rob told his friends, 'it's always a bit custardy just after calving, it's not allowed to be sold with all the rest.'

'If that's your calf's mum,' said Ian, 'where's its dad? It takes two to make a calf, doesn't it?'

'Come on then, I'll soon show you,' Rob said, turning eagerly to lead them off again. He had seen the bull so often himself that he had quite forgotten that his two friends had probably never seen him at all.

John was working half way down the byre, but he had kept his ears open. As the boys came running past he grabbed Rob by the arm and held him.

'Listen, now—no one goes in the bull's house, see? You can see him well enough through the bars.'

33

'Okay, John.'

They had to go out of the byre and across the inner yard. The bull had a big place to himself, all solid stone and iron bars. He had a thick brass ring in his nose and his name, Dewarch Prince, was on a steel plate fixed to the wall. He was eating steadily at his manger. Round it were iron bars instead of the stone wall, so they could have a good view of him.

'Jeepers,' cried Ian, 'just look at that *neck*!'

'Yes, he's big,' said Rob, 'one of the biggest we've ever had. He had horns once. Even John's feart of *him*.'

'But I bet the cows aren't,' said David. 'When does he go out? Oo, I'd love to see him prancing in the fields.'

'I don't think he does go in the fields now, ever,' said Rob rather sadly. 'Dad says bulls can't expect to, when they're grown-up, at least not dairy bulls. That's all old-fashioned.'

It was a very small birthday tea party this year. That was by Rob's own choice as well as his mother's, and it was because of what happened last year. He had had eight guests who after tea had rushed out into the steading and gone wild. John was away home by then and Rob's father had had to go into town, so there had been no one to keep the boys under control. Rob had done his best, but some of them were a year older than he and some of them had never been let loose on a farm before. And besides, he was feeling just as wild as they were.

34

There had been a stack of hay-bales in one of the yards, built in the open because there wasn't any more room in the barns. Being a temporary stack, put up in a hurry just before dark on a rainy summer night, it had a strong lean to one side and had been propped up with the trunk of a felled larch tree.

The boys had used this prop as a ladder and when they were all on it together it had broken clean through in the middle. They had all been thrown to the ground and then before they could get to their feet an avalanche of hay-bales had poured down on them.

By a stroke of luck no one had been really hurt. But Rob's father said it could have killed one of them and he and John were very upset about it, especially as it had rained in the night and some of the hay had been spoiled.

This year's party might be rather a quiet one, but it was not dull; certainly not for Rob, who was not going to find anything dull for a long time now that he had Temba, and not for David and Ian either because they had not been invited last year and so couldn't remember it. After tea the farmer took the boys to his big roll-top desk in his study to show them his herd-books and cattle register and how to make new entries in them for the new calf. Rob was allowed to write in Temba Dawn's name himself. How different it was from last year, when they all rushed out to the steading, yelling like a pack of wild animals! But it was good fun all the same and the day ended a lot more happily than it had the year before.

5
Halter Training

In a few days Rob had the feeding of Temba Dawn entirely in his own hands. He gave her five or six pints of Tarbo's milk, with a pint or so of hot water added, twice a day at half past seven in the morning and half past four in the afternoon. Whenever he entered her loose-box she came running to him. Within two days she could drink without a finger. At first he was pleased by that, but soon he began almost to regret it because the milk disappeared so quickly that it was hard to believe she had really had it. She found it hard to believe too.

He would have liked to continue with that simple routine, but his father said it was too expensive. At a gallon and a half a day she would be costing nearly a pound a week to keep. So milk-powder had to be added to her mother's milk, a bit more every day so that it would gradually replace fresh milk altogether. Milk-powder was made in factories and farmers could buy it cheaply in 100-pound bags. But it had to be mixed carefully with water. At first John had to help Rob to get it mixed really smoothly, for baby calves can get bad stomach troubles from swallowing lumps of powder.

Soon Temba was on milk substitute altogether and she didn't seem to notice the difference. Naturally Rob gave her a bit more of it than he was supposed to, certainly more than John was giving to the other young calves.

One Saturday morning when he was busy getting Temba clean (he had to scrub her back parts with warm water every two or three days) he heard his father and John in the neighbouring loose-box where the other three baby calves were. When he went to look over the half-door, there was John with one of the calves' heads gripped so tight between his knees and hands that it couldn't move an inch, while his father was operating on it with a red-hot iron. There was a little calor-gas cylinder beside them with a hissing flame and there was a strong smell of burned hair.

'What *are* you doing?' Rob asked accusingly.

'We're only de-horning 'em, son,' said his father. 'It's like going to the dentist—nasty, but necessary for your own good. We're coming to your Temba next.'

'*Oh*! Does it hurt?'

'No. We give 'em an injection, just like the dentist does for a big filling. You had one last time you went.' As he spoke he was burning off one of the calf's horn buds with the hot iron. Rob watched in fascinated horror.

'But some cows have horns, I saw some in Aberdeen market.'

'Oh, yes,' said his father. 'Some of the crofters stick to horns. If you only keep one or two cows, well, it's all right.'

'Dewarch had horns—why shouldn't Temba?'

His father finished the calf and straightened his back, looking thoughtfully at Rob while John released

37

that calf and seized hold of another.

'Well Rob, if you ever want to sell Temba you'll drop £10 at once if she's got horns. I bought Dewarch cheap because of those great sawn-off stumps he's got. They're dangerous.'

'Temba'll never be dangerous and I'll *never* sell her. I'd *like* her with horns, I think. She's *mine*.'

Rob saw his father exchange a wry smile with John. Then the farmer shrugged. 'All right, Rob, it can be your decision. But you can take my word for it, she'll be happier without 'em. When she's out in the fields in nine months' time, with a bunch of heifers of her own age, they'll all be lying down close together in a family circle, maybe, or standing packed together swinging their tails to keep off the flies—and if she's got horns on her she'll not be there, she'll be away outside the circle, she'll maybe not have a single friend—because they'll all be scared of her, you see. Isn't that right, John?'

'Ay,' said John, busy subduing the next calf.

So, very reluctantly, Rob had to agree to have Temba done. He knew his father was telling him the truth and, anyway, when it came to the point (he even helped to hold Temba during the operation) he realised that it couldn't be any worse for her than it had been for him in the dentist's chair a month ago. As he watched the needle go in with the injection of pain-killing stuff, he thought to himself, 'Well, *I* had to have that inside my mouth, she's only having it on the top of her head.'

It was a November Sunday afternoon before his father next found time to come and make a thorough inspection of Temba. He was extremely pleased.

'This is going to be a champion heifer,' he said as he ran his hand down her long straight back. 'Let's see, how old is she now?'

'Exactly five weeks, Dad.'

'Well, you're certainly doing her proud. You can try her with calf-nuts now, after every feed. Put a few in the bucket just as she's draining the last drop of milk out of it. And another thing you can do is, take her out for runs. I've got a calf-halter somewhere, that I daresay we can shorten a bit. Come into the harness room.'

There was a special little room near the bull's house that was still called that. It had an ancient stove and a chimney and was the place where for about two hundred years the harness of the farm horses (and there used to be a dozen at Tomallen) used to be looked after and mended. Today it was just a store-room, though in very cold weather the old stove was still sometimes used.

The farmer found a little halter, but when they put it on Temba it proved to be many sizes too big. 'That's what I feared, babies like this don't usually go out on halters, though it's really just what they need. If we tie a knot here perhaps we can make it fit.'

He tried again and it looked all right. So he gave the halter rope to Rob and opened the loose-box door.

'There you are, now the two of you can have the run of the yards, you can have the run of the whole farm if you like. But it'll take her a week or so to get the hang of it.'

Rob held on to the rope expectantly while Temba Dawn stood there looking through the open doorway. She took a step or two, with her head on one side, rather like a blackbird advancing on a worm. Two or three more dainty steps took her into the doorway where she could look a long way down a concrete passage leading to one of the byres. She was very interested indeed.

'Hold tight, she's away!' said the farmer warningly. He had seen her leg muscles tensing.

She charged out into the passage, dragging Rob behind her. After about ten yards he dug his heels in and brought her to such a sudden stop that her head and neck, pulled by the halter rope, went down on the concrete, her four legs came up into the air and she rolled on to her back, looking very surprised and silly. Rob thought she was hurt and gasped. But his father laughed.

'Just keep a firm hold of that rope and she'll get up when she's ready. It's her first fall and she's puzzled, but she'll have plenty like that. You mustn't lose hold of that rope whatever happens. You're her master, see?'

That was the beginning of wonderful times for Rob and his calf, especially at week-ends. She soon learned what the tug of the rope meant and though she fought with Rob many times, she always gave way in the end. He soon learned that she always *would* give way, it was part of her nature to do so.

She was extremely inquisitive. She wanted to go everywhere and there were only three places where he was forbidden to take her. One was into the byres when the cows were in, another was into any field where the cows were grazing, another was into the bull's house. Nothing had been said about the farmhouse, so one

Saturday morning he took her in through the back door into the scullery and then on into the kitchen.

He could hear his mother moving about in one of the sitting-rooms, so he called to her. Before she came in he pulled open the door of a big cupboard and made it swing right back in front of Temba, hiding her completely between it and the wall. When his mother entered he said,

'Shut your eyes, Mum.'

'Oh you—so you're up to one of your tricks again, are you? Well, all right, but only for a minute, I've got things in the oven to look at.'

'Now,' he said, 'give me your hand.'

He pulled her hand round quickly sideways and placed it fair and square over Temba's slobbery nose. Her nose was slobbery because the extremely warm kitchen had already made her sweat and cattle always sweat on their noses.

His mother let out such a yell that Temba took to her heels and dragged Rob out behind her through the scullery. He came very close to letting go of the rope on that occasion, because he was weak with laughter. After that there were four places where he was forbidden to take her.

What both Rob and Temba liked best was going out through the gate from the steading into the first big grass field and there taking off into a wild run. Living in that field were about a dozen yearling heifers, who at first quite often used to start running too, because they found it peculiar to see a baby calf going like the wind with a boy fastened on to her with a rope.

One of these yearlings was called Longmug because she had the longest face that had ever been seen on any animal at Tomallen Farm. She had been born with a long one and ever since it seemed to have grown a little bit faster than any other part of her body. Not that the rest of her had not grown fast too. It had indeed and she was now a lot bigger than she had any good reason to be. But her face had kept well ahead all the way. The farmer had been hoping for the past year that it would stop and let the rest of her catch up with it, but so far it had not. And so she had become a famous character at Tomallen, because she was highly intelligent too. Her brains at any rate must have kept pace with her face. But she was ugly, so ugly that people couldn't help smiling when they looked at her.

From the first moment when she saw them, Longmug took a special interest in Temba and Rob. She developed the habit of running level with them for a short distance, then putting on a sudden spurt and making rings round them, which her unusually long legs enabled her to do quite easily.

One cold Saturday in November, with white frost on the grass, when the three of them had been racing round the field and had come to a stop for breath, Longmug came up to Temba and licked her face. This gave Rob a chance to get close to Longmug, which he had never managed to do before. He smoothed his hand lightly up that incredibly long nose of hers, all the way up to the flat bony ridge of her forehead and then over the top and scratched with his fingers in the soft hollow down behind the ridge, midway between her two ears (and she had an outsize in ears too). His father had often told him that was what cows always liked, because it was the only piece of them that they couldn't lick or rub against a tree. Longmug liked it very much indeed.

So the three of them stood very close together for a while, as if they were making a pact of friendship. For Longmug, that was certainly just what it was. Rob and Temba couldn't know it, but in fact she had no friends at all. She was so much bigger than all the other yearlings that she bullied them without noticing it, always grabbing for herself the best patches of grass and the warmest places to lie in, out of the wind. And the others couldn't stand the length of her face, it gave them the willies. They never came close to her if they could avoid it.

Longmug's strange length of face did not worry Temba at all, because she had not met enough calves and heifers to know what was the proper size for their faces. Nor, of course, did it worry Rob, though he was glad his Temba did not have that sort of trouble. Temba was definitely pretty, both his father and John had agreed with him about that.

When Rob led Temba back to the steading that November morning, Longmug followed them and tried to come through the gate into the yard with them.

'Oh no,' said Rob firmly, 'I'm sorry, Longmug, you can't come in here, you'd only get me into trouble with John. If you want to be friends that's very much okay with us and we'll come and see you again tomorrow.'

He had to shut the gate in her face. As he and Temba went into the buildings out of her sight, she let out a

43

long complaining blare.

At dinner when Rob told about Longmug wanting to be friends, his father smiled.

'I can well believe it,' he said. 'That long-legged beastie is shaping up to be the most intelligent animal on the farm. She'll spoil the look of the herd and yet be a credit to it at the same time.'

Then after a minute he added,

'But that calf of yours has been alone in that loose-box quite long enough. It's time she had some company in there. Would you mind that?'

Rob had to do some thinking. It was nice of Dad to consult him about it, in fact it was typical of him, he seldom gave orders, either to Rob or to John, he just discussed things with them instead. But he nearly always got his own way.

After a minute's thought, Rob knew that he *would* mind not having his calf alone to himself in that loose-box any more, but he also knew that his father had already decided what would be best for Temba.

'Well, I don't know,' Rob said cautiously, 'I suppose it wouldn't be too bad if she just had *one* other in there with her—if you think she's really lonely.'

'She'll be happier that way,' said the farmer. 'All right then, you come along with me and we'll sort this out first thing after dinner.'

As Rob expected, his father took him straight to that other loose-box with the three calves in it.

'Now, I expect you've noticed that one of these is different, haven't you?'

'Different?' repeated Rob blankly. He had been so

taken up with Temba Dawn that he had not bothered to pay close attention to any of these.

'Yes, different,' said his father a trifle impatiently. 'Look at 'em now and surely you can see it?'

Just at that moment one of them, which had just got to its feet when they entered, started making water and Rob couldn't fail to notice that the water came out nearly half way along its under-belly instead of between its hind legs. Then he understood suddenly how slow in the uptake he had been.

'Oh, so that one's a bull!'

'Of course it is, you nitwit!' The farmer gave his son a playful punch. 'Can't you see what a much broader head he's got? His mother's the best milker we've ever had, so we're going to keep this little chap and raise him to take the place of Dewarch Prince. How do you think your Temba will like that? To be raised in the company of another prince?'

'Oo, that's great!' said Rob. 'Only—how soon will he get tough?'

'If he's treated right he needn't ever get tough at all, I'm aiming to make him into a really tame and friendly bull, not at all like Dewarch Prince who's soon likely to get too difficult for us to manage. Dewarch wasn't born on this farm, you know. Now, you run and fetch your calf's halter and we'll shift this little man into Temba's box right away.'

The bull-calf's name, Rob's father told him, was Rombold the Second.

'He hasn't got his ear-tag on yet, because we've been waiting to see how he shapes in his first two months.

45

But I can decide now that he'll do—he'll do just fine.'

'What about his nose-ring?' Rob asked.

'Och, he won't get that till he's a year old. Now, open the door and hold back those two lassies and we'll see what Rombold says to a bit of freedom.'

Rombold was so big and strong that the farmer had to struggle and wrestle with him all the way to Temba's box. Once they had him inside they stood to watch while the two calves smelled and licked each other.

'Supposing they fight?' Rob asked anxiously.

But it was plain they were delighted with each other. His father told him that according to his experience very young animals never fight, except in play. 'They seem better tempered than children,' he said, giving his son a grin.

6

The Mating of Tarbo

It was a Sunday morning at the beginning of December. Something had woken Rob early, while it was still pitch dark. He lay in bed listening and thinking.

He did not really want to get up, nor did he want any more sleep. So he switched on the light over his bed and reached for the book he was in the middle of. It was glossy and lovely to handle because it was new, although it was not his own but out of the school library. The English teacher had advised him to ask for it, knowing it had just come in, and he was the first to borrow it. It was about a Kodiak bear-cub. An American boy in Alaska had found it, out in the wilds clinging to its dead mother. Somebody had shot the mother because Kodiaks are so dangerous, the biggest and fiercest bears in the world. But the boy took the cub home with him and made it into a pet and became rather famous, because of course it grew up long before he did and yet he could still lead it about on a rope when it weighed about 400 pounds and stood eight feet tall on its hind legs.

All the same he couldn't get on with the story this morning because he kept hearing again the noise that had probably awakened him—a cow blaring from the byres. But why should that wake him when it was one of the most ordinary of all the farm noises? Well, for one

47

thing, it was unusually loud and urgent in tone, and for another it was vaguely familiar.

Suddenly he knew it was Tarbo's voice calling. What could be wrong with her, had she suddenly remembered Temba Dawn after all this time or could she somehow have caught sight of her or smelled her?

He got out of bed, went to the window and opened it a bit. By putting his head close to the glass he could see the lights streaming out from the byres, the dairy and the yards. He could hear better too. Yes, he decided, things were not normal this morning. First, there was snow on the ground, about two inches at least, and second, the bull as well as Tarbo was blaring, using all the higher ranges of his voice, not roaring but calling.

Then Rob heard the muffled tramp of feet over the snow and men's voices at the back door. His father must be downstairs talking to John. He thought John mentioned Tarbo's name, then he heard his father call out, 'Better wait for me, I'll be with you in two to three minutes.'

So Rob threw his clothes on quick and ran down just in time to catch the farmer putting on his rubber boots in the scullery.

'What's up, Dad? Can I come?'

'It's just Tarbo bulling. We've been trying to catch her right day for a longish time now. Yes, all right, you've got to see it sooner or later. But you must keep out of the way.'

The milking herd had been lying in at night since late November. The byres were warm and steamy, with a smell of cow so strong you could almost cut it with a knife. Rob liked it well enough. He followed his father into the first of the byres, where Tarbo's stall was. John had finished with the milking, but a good half of the morning's routine work still remained to be done.

After calling to John, the farmer walked up close to Tarbo and had a good look at her. At that moment she arched her back and blared so loudly that some white-wash flaked off from a roof-beam over her head and fluttered down like an autumn leaf. Then she stretched her head right round and sniffed at her hinder parts, her eyes looking very big and dark. The bull called again in answer to her blare.

'Right!' shouted the farmer to John. 'I'm going to turn her loose. Rob, you run and open the gate into the inside yard and stay by it.'

As soon as Tarbo was untied she hurried out of the byre and down the passage and through the gate into the inside yard.

'Shut the gate now,' called the farmer to Rob as the two men went to get Dewarch Prince. John tipped some cow-cake into the bull's manger from outside, through the bars, to entice him into the corner where the man-ger was, then as soon as he started eating the farmer entered his house carrying the bull-stick (a very strong thick staff about five feet long with a spring clip on one end). While the bull was still eating the farmer reached right forward into his manger and clipped the end of the stick through his nose-ring. The minute that was done, the bull was firmly under control, so the farmer was able to pull his great head round sideways and lead him out by a second door opening directly into the yard.

It was plain to Rob that that was just what Dewarch wanted to do, because he knew there was a cow there waiting for him.

The bull walked straight up to Tarbo, sniffing and snorting. She touched noses with him, then turned her back on him and took a few steps away.

Rob had been told to stay out of the yard behind the gate that he had just shut, but he climbed two bars of it and hung over its top so as to be able to watch everything better. His father was standing beside Dewarch, gripping the bull-stick with both hands but not pulling on it, just taking its weight so that it wouldn't worry the bull. Tarbo kept on taking a few steps away, but looking over her shoulder most of the time, nervous but not scared. Every time the bull walked after her the farmer had to move too, of course. Rob could see that Dewarch was well accustomed to being held on the stick; he wasn't giving it a moment's thought. Rob could also see that it wasn't at all like that for his father, who was watching the bull closely and thinking about him as hard as Tarbo must be.

Was it the enormous size of Dewarch that was making everything tense and a bit frightening? Rob couldn't help wondering what would happen if an animal like that, so obviously built for strength, got really angry. And yet he had seen bigger things in a zoo, an elephant and a giraffe for instance, and he did not remember wondering the same thing about them. Perhaps he was uneasy because he had so often heard his father talk about bulls being dangerous, or because John was so strict about keeping people out of Dewarch's house.

However it was, being a little scared made it all a lot more interesting.

As soon as Tarbo finally consented to stand still, Dewarch mounted her. Rob was amazed by the ease and the speed of it. One moment the bull was standing there as solidly planted on his four legs as a great oak tree in a field, and the next there he was on his hind legs with those mountainous shoulders of his right up over the top of Tarbo's back and the hooves of his forelegs pressing into her sides. Rob had seen animals riding each other often enough before. He had seen cows doing it, and heifers and big calves doing it, and of course dogs and poultry. So he had expected and been waiting for the bull to ride Tarbo. But there were two things he had not expected. One was, that Dewarch did it in such an easy swinging way, without any effort, although it looked so difficult and awkward beforehand, and the other was, that the farmer put out a hand (leaving only one for the bull-stick) and pulled the cow's tail to one side so that the bull could get his penis into the right place more easily. Rob hadn't expected his father actually to give Dewarch a helping hand with the job.

The bull stayed mounted only half a minute. Just when Tarbo's legs began trembling, as if they were going to buckle under the weight, Dewarch gave a big final lunge that pushed Tarbo out from under him, so that he came down with a bang on to his front legs again.

The farmer at once pulled his nose round towards the door he had come out by and got him slowly on the move. John arrived at that moment to help, prodding

51

Dewarch from behind. Rob was relieved to see him being led back quietly into his house. He did however stop at the doorway and swing his head round for a last look at Tarbo. The farmer tried to stop that head-swing but failed—and the bull raised his nose to let out one high-pitched bellow. So the two men shouted very loudly at him, both together, giving him resounding smacks with their hands on his flanks.

Dewarch knew well what they wanted and gave way, knowing there was unfinished food waiting for him in his manger. Rob watched his eyes, trying to think his thoughts for him. It was obvious there *were* thoughts going on behind that massive bulldozer forehead.

He couldn't be thinking *only* about Tarbo. If he wanted so badly to stay with her, wouldn't he also be having thoughts about the two men who were preventing it? Angry thoughts? No, just resigned and sad ones, it seemed to Rob. Why? Where did the power of those two men come from, really? With one good lunge of his head, Dewarch could crush them both to death against a wall. Rob pretended hard to be Dewarch and then took another long look at his father and John. He would have to look *up* at them, they were both tall, well above the level of Dewarch's eyes. Was that part of the secret? If they were on all fours, like Dewarch—oh, what would be left of their power then?

Rob got off his gate and ran round to the corner bars close to the bull's manger, where he could see through and watch Dewarch being brought back into his house. As soon as the farmer unclipped the stick from his nose, the bull went to his manger and Rob found himself within two feet of that mighty head; its sawn-off horns were like old chopping-blocks, tough as iron, yet worn down by constant bashing. Its eyes were like deep dark pools, with things moving under the surface. He could just see himself reflected in those eyes. Were they looking at him? No, they were just passing over him, busy with other thoughts.

His father and John, coming out of the bull's house together, smiled to see Rob still there, still studying Dewarch's face as he ate at his manger.

'Well, there you are, son. That's the way it's done. We write in the date now on Tarbo's stall and then if she's not blaring for Dewarch again in three weeks' time we'll know she's started a calf.'

Then he turned and said to John,

'I wish I knew what that bull was thinking. Because I reckon he *does*, a fair bit. What do you say, John?'

'Ay,' said John. 'He thinks. There's nae wickedness in him yet—but I'll nae be sayin' it winna come.'

7
The Visitors

From that time on, Temba Dawn had three playmates,
Rob, Rombold and Longmug. She was one of the hap-
piest calves in the world and so she ought to be, for
certainly no other heifer calf had ever been so well
treated and well fed as she. Rob discovered at once that
Rombold, because he was being reared as a bull, was
still having whole milk instead of milk-powder and
would continue having it, regardless of expense, for
another three or four months. So naturally Rob begged
his father to let Temba have some whole milk too, even
if it was only once a day, and his father gave way. It was
a fair exchange between the two calves; Temba got one
of Rombold's privileges for being a bull and he got
some of her privileges for being Rob's pet.

It very soon became necessary for Rob to start train-
ing Rombold too with a halter, though in a more cautious way according to his father's instructions. A second
halter was provided and then every time he went to the
loose-box to take Temba out he first of all tied Rombold
to an iron ring in the wall. That was partly to make it possible for him and Temba to get out through the door and
leave Rombold behind, and partly to get the bull-calf
well broken-in to the feel of the halter before ever being
taken out of the box at all. Because he was so strong
(and all that whole milk he had had was partly res-

54

ponsible for that), *his* walks and runs would have to come later, when he would have learned that he could not overcome the rope that held him.

Temba and Rombold grew very fast, but also very evenly, not at all like poor Longmug with her outsize face. They both had shining eyes and shining coats as well as tremendous appetites. Besides their usual foods, milk, calf-nuts, hay and silage, Rob brought them all kinds of luxuries from the farmhouse garden, things like cabbages, carrots, broccoli leaves and apples. They were both crazy about apples. He even tried them sometimes with cooked potatoes from the kitchen, which they ate doubtfully but decided to like. With his father's help he fixed up a salt-lick for them, to supply them with any minerals they might possibly be short of. Very often he found one or the other of them licking away at it with as much enjoyment as a kid with an ice-cream cone, so much so that he had to keep on renewing it.

When December came he couldn't take Temba out either before or after school, it was too dark. He couldn't even see her by daylight except at week-ends and even then it wasn't so much fun in the fields as it used to be because of snow and hail and slush and mud and very cold hands and feet.

One Saturday morning he got out into the fields with her and then found that he had left his gloves behind. Because it was so cold she wanted to race, so he had to hold very tight on the halter rope or she would have broken away from him. Gripping the rope so tight made his hands colder and colder until they began to hurt really badly. He hated to disappoint Temba and end

55

her usual long Saturday run so early. Nor did he want to disappoint Longmug, who was in a great running mood that morning. He felt pretty certain that for both of them these runs together in the field were the best things in their lives at this dark time of the year. So he stuck it out as long as he could and when he got back to the loose-box his hands had gone thoroughly queer, sort of half dead but still hurting. He had to go and hold them under the hot tap in the scullery. That made them hurt far more at first, until he was almost screaming over them. His mother told him he ought to have had more sense. If your hands start to hurt with cold you've got to do something about it at once or you'll be in trouble. After that he kept a spare pair of gloves in a pocket of his anorak.

Then it was suddenly Christmas time and school holidays were starting in two days and his parents at breakfast were opening a letter and saying, 'Oh good, they can come.'

'When?'

'They're taking the night-boat tomorrow.'

They were special friends of Rob's parents, a married couple who had one daughter and lived in the Orkney Islands. They had come to stay at Tomallen once before about two years ago. Ever since then Rob knew that his parents had been keen for them to come again, because he was an only child and knew almost nothing about girls. Their daughter Kirsty was also an only child.

'What do you say to that, Rob?' his mother asked and he didn't have an answer ready. Two years was a long time and he needed first to draw a picture in his mind of Kirsty's face and general shape. Freckles, he remembered, and ginger hair, lots of puffy bouncing ginger hair and rather long greenish eyes under it, with a teasing glint in them. Also long legs, thin but fast. He had not been able to beat her at running. Yes, she had been quite a person, though perhaps a little bit superior, a little bit too keen on clean clothes. He didn't really want anything or anybody else just now, when he had Temba and Rombold and Longmug, but it would be fun to show them all to Kirsty.

'How long for, Mum?'

'Oh, about a week. Perhaps till after hogmanay. Depends when school starts again in Kirkwall.'

'Where'll she sleep?' He remembered giving up his bed to her last time and making do with a mattress on the floor. He had enjoyed that because it seemed like camping out.

'She's nearly twelve now. We can put another bed in the guest-room and she can sleep with her parents.'

'Oh, what a shame,' said Rob.

'We'll give her a choice then,' said his mother. 'If you want to give up your bed to her again you can.'

'I know what her parents will try to make her choose,' said the farmer with a smile. 'They'll want the guest-room to themselves.'

Kirsty's father was a bank clerk, but as he had been brought up on a farm he was always very pleased to come and stay on one. For Kirsty and her mother it was the other way about. They liked Tomallen because you could get into Aberdeen from it in about fifteen minutes and after Kirkwall they found it thrilling to be in a big city.

So the first two days of Kirsty's visit had to be taken up with Christmas shopping in the city. Rob's mother expected him to go too, which meant that he had very little time left for Temba Dawn. Kirsty could not go out into the yards at all, since she was always wearing her best clothes.

On the morning of the third day Rob began to feel really fed up. He liked Kirsty very much indeed, but that only made it worse. How could such a nice sensible girl think it more fun to go traipsing endlessly round Aberdeen buying clothes than to go out and be introduced to Temba Dawn and Rombold and Longmug, to say nothing of Tarbo and Dewarch and John? This third morning he had got up at his usual time and slipped out without waking her and gone to feed Temba and Rombold and now he had just come back quietly into his room to get tidy for breakfast.

It was half past eight and nearly daylight, but she was still asleep! She didn't appear to have moved an inch since he had peeped at her in the light of his electric torch half an hour ago. He was peeping at her with it now, but her eyes were under the bedclothes. It was really too much. It was *his* room and he had been afraid even to switch the light on.

He went out on to the landing and down two or three stairs, then came up again as loudly as he could, stamping and whistling, hitting his door wider open with his fist and switching on the light over the bed. Then he stamped across the room to draw back the window-curtains with a flourish.

When he turned, Kirsty was sitting up in bed gaping at him, her eyes long green slits under an untidy mass of ginger curls.

'You *are* a sleepy thing!' he said accusingly. 'I've been out to Temba ages ago and you haven't met her even *yet*!'

She only stared at him as if she'd never seen him before. It was so obvious that she had been a long way away and needed a bit of time for the return journey that he began to feel less cross. And her face, after all, was quite as attractive as Temba's.

'Oh, I was—' she tried to speak but was stopped by a huge yawn. 'I was having a dream. I think I was—at a pantomime. Oh yes—Rob, we're going to one on Tuesday, aren't we?'

'I suppose so,' he said. 'We usually do, at Christmas. It was *Peter Pan* last year and the crocodile was great. But it wasn't *real*. I like *real* animals, don't you?'

She wrinkled her nose at him. 'You've got real-animal smell on you. Is that your Temba Dawn's smell?' She pointed to his anorak that he was just unzipping. When he had slipped his arms out of it he held it first to his own nose and then over the bed to hers.

'Yes,' she said, sniffing hard. 'Well, I suppose it's not bad really. Only a bit strong for a bedroom.'

'Might be for yours,' he said, 'not for mine. It's milk, mostly, with a bit of silage to it, an' p'rhaps a whiff or two of linseed cake. Might be just a teeny whiff of dung, but I always leave my boots in the scullery.'

'Oh well,' she said, very soon bored with the subject,

59

'I'm going to the bathroom.'

She threw back the bedclothes and jumped out, enjoying his interested gaze.

He followed her hopefully. Really he found her as interesting as Temba, but he was not yet willing to admit that, even to himself.

'Will you come out on the farm this morning? And put on old clothes?' he asked anxiously.

'No, I can't, we're going to the Art Gallery. Mummy promised to take me because art's my special subject at school. You're coming too I think.'

'Oh flippin' heck—no, I'm not—I *must* take Temba out, she hasn't had a proper run since you came.'

He was so disgusted that he turned and left her, forgetting to wash, and ran down to breakfast to complain about it to his mother.

But he did go to the Art Gallery with Kirsty and her mother that morning after all, because Kirsty promised she really would at last go out on the farm with him in the afternoon. What is more, he found it well worth going, because there was one picture there that worked a strange fascination over him. While the three of them were in the Gallery he kept on returning to look at it, almost getting lost by the other two several times, and when they got home he talked to his father about it during dinner-time.

When he said it was much the biggest picture in the whole show, his father said with a chuckle,

'Oh, so you would buy your pictures by the square yard, would you?'

'Oh Dad, really! No, but you ought to see this one,

60

it's terrific—it's all animals, sheep an' cows an' horses an' goats—an' dogs an' cats—all with awful fear in their faces and sort of drowning in a great storm. There are people too, on the roof of their house, with trees blowing down and water swirling round 'em everywhere. It's terrific, Dad, really it is.'

His parents looked at him with surprised smiles, then turned to Kirsty for her opinion.

'I couldn't bear it,' she said. 'It makes you cry. I just want to forget it, only I can't. But anyway it's not by one of the real *top* painters, is it, Mummy?'

'It's a Landseer,' said her mother. 'He was a Victorian, so people don't think much of him today. But it's a picture no one's ever likely to forget. Tell them about the one *you* like so much, Kirsty.'

Kirsty blushed and looked down into her lap. 'Well, it's just a girl, in a red dress and cloak, who looks—all by herself.' Then Kirsty suddenly found courage and flashed a bold glance all round the table. 'You see, she looks so certain she's right and that everything belongs to her—for ever. And she must have been a real person, mustn't she? Oh, how I'd love to know what sort of life she had.'

'That was a Millais,' said her mother. 'Another Victorian. Aberdeen is rather a Victorian place, at least it was till this oil boom started.'

8

Rombold's First Run

As soon as Rob and Kirsty entered the loose-box, the two calves scrambled to their feet and ran up to them. They had brought some cabbage leaves for them, which were quickly eaten. Rob stood stroking Temba under her chin and down the front of her neck, which she specially liked, but he was watching Kirsty to see if she was scared at all. She certainly was not.

'So *that*'s your Temba Dawn,' she said, copying Rob's stroking actions. 'Isn't she dark and shiny? Oh, she's slobbering over my hand. I must say she smells rather nice.'

'She probably thinks *we* do, too,' said Rob. 'Do you think she's prettier than Rombold?'

Kirsty turned her attention to the bull-calf, rubbing a hand over his head, but he butted it roughly away.

'No,' said Rob quickly, 'they don't like being touched on the top, only underneath. You'll soon find that out.'

Kirsty smoothed her hand under Rombold's chin and then all the way down to his chest, which was like a white shirt-front. He lifted his nose and gave her a very wet lick on the face.

'Rombold *isn't* pretty,' she said, 'he's noble, like his name. They're beautifully clean, aren't they?'

'That's because I give them lots of straw,' said Rob. 'And that makes the floor get higher and higher. John says he'll have to muck it all out soon and start again or else we'll be scraping our heads on the roof.'

They didn't talk for a while after that. Rob was busy thinking, Kirsty was busy making friends with Rombold and getting the feel of the farm buildings, in which there was a good deal of clatter going on because John was getting ready the cows' evening meal.

Being very keen to make Kirsty's first afternoon on the farm really interesting, Rob was thinking out some way of doing it. Why shouldn't this be the opportunity for Rombold to have his first run in the fields? There would be two of them to hold the rope, in case he got over-excited. But it might be a good thing to consult John about it first.

'Would you rather be a farmer or an artist, when you grow up?' Kirsty suddenly asked, making Rob's train of thought come to a dead stop and start off in a new direction.

'An artist? D'you mean a *painter*? Is that what *you* want to be?'

'I'd like to, yes, if I can. To make pictures that'll last a hundred years, perhaps a hundred years after I'm dead. It *would* be super, don't you think?'

Rob was too busy thinking to have anything to say.

'Of course animals are nice,' she continued, still smoothing her hands over Rombold, 'but they keep dying, or getting killed. They don't *last*.'

'Well, I want to be out of doors,' said Rob. 'Either farming or foresting. Yes, I'd like to be a forest-warden and drive for miles and miles over mountains in a land-rover.'

63

chased by a wolf or a tiger or something and they fled away in a wide circle round the field, some of them taking flying leaps sideways and kicking up their hind-legs just for the fun of it.

When Rob managed to bring Temba to a stop, which he could do as soon as they reached the place where some of the hay was still lying and making the ground firmer, all the heifers came round in a circle and stood still too, snorting and sniffing.

'That big one's Longmug,' said Rob.

Kirsty had a good look, then burst out laughing, but it was a silvery affectionate sort of laugh that Rob was pleased with. Surely that wouldn't hurt Longmug's feelings—or could it?

'I see what you mean,' said Kirsty. 'Oh, poor Long-mug. I mustn't laugh, must I? But it's such a funny face, there's miles of it. Do you think she knows?'

Longmug had come right up to them now and was licking Temba's neck. Both children started smoothing their hands over Longmug, who seemed to like it.

'You see, she's absolutely tame,' Rob said as he handled one of her outsize hairy ears to show Kirsty her metal ear-tag.

'That's only her number,' said Kirsty. 'Is Longmug *really* her name?'

'Oh yes, because you see she's had that sort of face all the way up, from being born. There's nothing *wrong* with her, Dad says, or he'd never have kept her. She's just a rather special sort of character.'

'How old is she?'

'Over a year, but I'm not sure how much. All those

66

are about the same age, only she's by far the biggest. They all have heat periods every three weeks and ride each other like mad.'

Temba was soon off again, with Longmug as well as Rob running beside her. After three days without a run she had big reserves of energy to use up.

But the afternoon was closing in. It would get dark so early these days and Rob needed plenty of daylight for Rombold.

'I tell you what we'll do,' he said. 'We'll take Temba back now and let her loose in the inner yard, where the bull serves the cows. She can stay there till we've done Rombold. She can't get out, it's sure to be all right.'

Why ever hadn't he thought of that before? When they pushed her through the gate and took her halter off, she obviously got a special thrill from running without it, all by herself. She went round the yard in fine style, making the bull bellow as she scampered past his window.

The next thing was to find John, but that wasn't so easy. They hunted all through the byres and the barns without finding any trace of him.

'He must have gone out to the fields then,' said Rob gloomily. 'And he probably won't be back till he brings the cows in, when it's nearly dark. Oh heck, I wish I'd asked him before.'

'Well, come on, let's do it,' said Kirsty. 'There's two of us, after all.'

Rob was doubtful of it, but they were already at the open loose-box door where they could see Rombold standing patiently inside, tied to the iron ring but watching them expectantly. Then Rob had a good idea. He put Temba's halter as well on the bull-calf, so that they would be able to hold him one from each side. Then he untied the rope and the three of them went out into the passage.

Rombold was cautious at first. He walked slowly, looking about him with great interest. When they got him to the gate into the field he stopped to call to Temba not knowing what had become of her. But as soon as he was through the gateway and into the field, feeling soft grass under his feet for the first time in his life, he went off at a fast trot, which developed into a mad gallop.

Rob and Kirsty only just managed to hold him. On all the slippery patches they tried the ski-ing process again, which worked even better than before now that they had a rope on each side of their calf.

The heifers all galloped too, of course, until Rombold stopped for his first rest, when they all came up close to examine him, led as usual by Longmug.

'We've got him now,' Rob said when he had breath enough to speak.

After giving him a good sniffing-over and a lick or two, Longmug suddenly reared up and got her front legs astride of him. She was so much bigger and heavier than he that he crumpled on to the ground and then scrambled out frantically from underneath her and set off into another mad gallop. This time he went even faster, as if she had frightened or offended him. She came after him, close on his heels, and was certainly gaining on him. The children could see that she intended to ride him again and that, to prevent it, they

would need to do something at once, either make Rombold swerve or double back sideways or else—good
heavens, he was going to do a third thing, he was
charging straight at the fence!

They realised, in horror, as they dug their heels in
and slithered to a stop, pulling back in vain on their
halter ropes, that he could not know what a wire fence
was, for he had never seen or felt one at close quarters.
This fence, luckily, was made mostly of plain wire.
Only the top strand was barbed and none of the wires
were stretched very tight.

Because of his speed, which he did not slacken at all
as he approached the fence, Rombold's head and shoulders went right through between the middle strands of
plain wire and somehow his legs and body had to follow.
On the other side he dived on to his nose and went
slithering down a steep bank into the next field, with
his two ropes trailing on the ground behind him. The
children had been forced to let go.

They could do nothing but gaze after him in astonishment, as all the heifers did. He went away at a steady
trot across that other field, which had been recently
ploughed and was all furrows of bare sticky brown earth.

Kirsty let out yells. 'Rob, run after him—run—run—
oh Rob, look, he's away—'

When things went wrong Rob seldom spoke, he only
went white and frowning, very intense and thinking. So
he was not quick in emergencies, but neither was he ever
silly.

He went up to the fence to handle the plain wire
strands, which were a good deal slacker than they had

been before. Then he went to the nearest post, which was leaning badly, and pushed it back upright.

'It's nae too bad,' he said, looking at the interested line of heifers. 'Those are bigger, they'll not be able to follow him.'

Kirsty was almost wringing her hands. 'What a' we going to *do*, Rob, how'll we ever get him *back*?'

'Och, don't get so daft, Kirsty.' As he spoke he was climbing through the fence. 'We'll just go after him slowly, if he's so scared it'll nae be any good running.'

Rombold had gone across the middle of the ploughed field, towards a hedge on the farther side. When the children reached the hedge they saw there was an open gate in it, leading into a wood. There was no sign of Rombold.

As soon as they were among the trees, Rob stopped still and put a finger to his lips. 'Sh-shush, Kirsty, let's listen.'

It was a very still afternoon. They could hear the traffic on the road to the city, the cackle of a hen from behind the steading and then Dewarch's voice calling to Temba. But at first not a sound from the wood.

Then they both noticed a faint tearing and rustling from somewhere close and a moment later they saw a dark shape moving slowly behind clumps of bramble. It was Rombold eating, enjoying some fresh grass that hadn't been grazed since the summer. They were able to creep up on him and grab the halter ropes. These were in a sad state, coated with mud and frayed at the ends where he had repeatedly stepped on them.

He was perfectly calm again, but they could see he

70

was rather the worse for wear. He had a red gash on his forehead, where the wire had scraped off some skin, and a nasty long raw scrape on one leg.

'There,' said Rob, leaning on the calf and giving a long sigh of relief, 'he's seen a bit of life, but he's going home now, at once. John's got some special stuff to put on raw places like that.'

9
The Staggering News

Kirsty's visit had come and gone all too quickly, the holidays were over, it was towards the end of January and the weather had been beastly. Neither of the calves had had a run for almost a week. But it was a Saturday, so when Rob was asked at breakfast what he intended to do with his morning he naturally mentioned Temba Dawn and Rombold. The bull-calf had become by this time as easy to lead about the farm as Temba. He had learned, in the hard way, what fences were and now he would not willingly go near one. Rob had been forbidden to take him again into the field where Longmug and the heifers were, but apart from that neither his father nor John had made any objections to Rob taking him out as often as he liked. They said it would greatly help in making Rombold a tame and friendly bull for the rest of his life.

This morning Rob had already noticed that his father had just had a letter that made him think very hard and very seriously. So although there was something Rob intended to ask, he had been putting it off all through breakfast until his mother started him talking about the calves. At last he asked it.

'Dad, will it be all right to take Rombold into the paddock to see the three heifers?'

His father collected his thoughts from a long way off,

such a long way that he seemed not to have heard his son's question, but only his voice.

'There are some very important things I have to tell you, Rob. I think it would be a good idea for me to come out on the farm with you, this morning. I'll take the bull-calf and you take your Temba Dawn and we'll do a tour of the whole farm, shall we?'

'Oo, yes—that'll be great, Dad.'

His father hadn't seen either of the calves lately. He had been going into Aberdeen nearly every day on business which seemed to be worrying and upsetting him pretty thoroughly. Now he was smiling, but Rob suspected he was putting on an act, or perhaps just making the most of these two calves so as to forget what was gnawing at him.

'Well, little man,' he said to Rombold, 'your sore places have healed well, haven't they? I expect that heifer's been licking them for you. And as for *you*, Temba Dawn, my goodness, you *are* a little glamour-girl, aren't you? Just look at those long dark eyelashes. Yes, you've got two champion calves here, son, that's as plain as daylight.'

'Since you're coming with us, Dad, can we go into Longmug's field? I bet she's longing to see Rombold again.'

The farmer smiled and gave his son a searching look. 'You can't bear these calves to get bored, Rob, can you? You really seem to feel for them. Well, yes, all right, we'll let 'em meet again, but if she tries riding him again I'll have to get tough with her.'

Since Rob's father had no intention of running, the

visit fell rather flat. The four of them stood in a bunch by the gate and allowed the heifers, led by Longmug, to come up and sniff at them and have polite conversation with them. It gave the farmer a chance to make an estimate of how each heifer was growing and how soon she ought to be put to the bull.

'Hm, yes, Longmug's ready,' he said. 'And the sooner we get *her* in calf the better. Oh no you don't, you silly old beggar.'

He had to give her a quick blow on the nose with his fist, because she was already too close to the bull-calf and her front legs were showing a tendency to lift off the ground. She gave up at once and stood quietly, as if she knew perfectly well that she couldn't get away with it a second time.

So there was a silence, at the end of which the farmer said, in an altogether different tone of voice,

'Well now, Rob, *this* is the serious thing I have to say to you. We have got to sell Tomallen. We have got to go.'

He had his head turned away so that Rob could not see his face, but his voice was peculiar, much thicker than usual, husky, as if he had a bad cold.

Rob was much too surprised to speak.

His father continued, 'I've been given warnings once or twice. I never took them seriously enough, but now it's all going to happen—all the land round here is wanted for houses and factories, there's a whole new town planned out and our farm is right plumb in the middle of it. They'll pay us well to go, but—I don't want to. By God, no, I don't want to.'

74

After another silence, Rob managed to say,

'D'you mean, Dad, take all the cows and heifers and everything somewhere else?'

'No, I mean sell everything and try another job. Your mother and I have been discussing it for days and days—and we think that's best. The letter I had this morning confirms it.'

'Where will we live then? In a town? In Aberdeen? Where will I keep Temba?'

Rob was doing his best to hold his voice down to its usual level, but there was something pushing it up from below.

'That will be worked out later, Rob. There's a good chance you can keep Temba if we can get a house in the country with a wee bit of grassland tacked on to it.'

That stopped Rob from speaking, for it was the worst he had heard yet. When grown-ups said, 'There's a good chance this will happen' or 'There's a good chance you'll be able to do that', it usually meant that they had decided on something thoroughly horrible. 'A good chance' really meant 'a faint hope'. And as for 'an excellent chance', that was even worse, that meant 'a very faint hope'.

'Dad, is Temba mine? Did you really give her to me?'

This time Rob's voice was firm and hard. It was a bit high, but not shamefully high. He was satisfied with it. It proved effective, too, for his father turned at last and looked squarely at him.

'Of course she's yours, Rob.'

'Can anyone *make* me sell her?'

'No, son, no one can do that.'

75

'Can anyone take her away from me by force?'

'Legally, perhaps *I* can, but I shall not. No one else can, unless you're ill-treating her in some way.'

Rob gave a sigh of relief. 'That's all right then. You see, I promised I'd look after her, all her life.'

'A rash promise, Rob. She may live ten or twelve years. Just think of yourself at twenty-two years old. You may be in New Zealand, you may be on the moon. Things move fast you know, these days, Temba could be a millstone round your neck.'

'But I promised, Dad!' He was holding his calf's head against his chest, stroking her neck. She was enjoying it so much that she had closed her eyes. In fact she looked really soppy.

The farmer was doing the same to the bull-calf, though absent-mindedly. He was evidently having very hard and difficult thoughts, just as his son was. There was a long silence except for the snuffling and sniffing and fidgeting of the animals.

'But Dad,' Rob said at last, 'what about Rombold? D'you mean he'll never be the Tomallen bull now, he'll never take Dewarch's place?'

'Ay, that's sad,' said the farmer, shaking his head. 'But he'll make a grand bull for some other farm. Maybe he'll just be old enough to give your Temba a calf, before we go.'

'When will we be going then?'

'We've got till the end of the year. We'll be having a live-and-dead stock sale here, like the one we went to at Meldrum last autumn, you remember? October will be the best month for that. These two should be old enough for breeding by then—certainly Rombold will, though Temba may be a bit on the young side.'

After a few moments Rob said, in a tone of voice he didn't like the sound of, 'That means we've got eight months—and then everything will be gone. There won't *be* any Tomallen Farm any more.'

'That's it, Rob. That's what life is, some things finishing but other things starting. *Everything* comes to an end, the good things as well as the bad. Childhood does, too, sooner than most. This lot of heifers are nearly finished with theirs. Certainly *that* thing is, if she ever really had one.'

He pointed at Longmug and smiled. But it was not his usual smile. Glancing at it sideways, Rob found it so little like his father's usual one that he could not return it.

They did have their walk round the farm, with the two calves beside them, but it was only the calves who enjoyed it. There was a freezing wind blowing, moaning in the bare trees and with flakes of snow in it now and then. The cows had given up trying to find any grass worth eating and were standing all together in a huddle by the gate, waiting for evening milking-time.

'Could be a month's snow coming,' said the farmer, gazing at the darkening sky. They hardly spoke again until they were putting the calves back in their loose-box. By then it was nearly dark and John could be heard bringing home the cows. The farmer hurried away to help him, so Rob was left alone in the only place where he wanted to be.

He sat down on an old milking stool that he had

found in the harness-room and that he now kept in the calves' box, hung up out of their reach. It would help him with all the alterations he had to make in his thoughts and feelings. He needed time and solitude to deal with them. No, not solitude, because he had the calves for company, but the absence of humans. No, not the absence of humans either, because he would like Kirsty to be there again, but the absence of grown-ups.

Now that he was going to lose it, he was discovering what it was he really most liked and wanted when he looked into the future. It was, to go on being a special person at Tomallen Farm, the farmer's son who could go everywhere and do everything, in all those buildings and all over those fields and woods, so long as he kept to the rules, and invite his friends and Kirsty to come and share them and have them all explained to them by him.

Yes, and not only to be a special person at Tomallen, but also to have two other special people, Temba and Rombold, as his closest friends. Well, to have Kirsty too, of course.

Yes, that had been his idea of the future. To have the farm there all the time as a steady interesting background, with specially good things cropping up in it every now and then, another visit from Kirsty, for instance, or turning Temba and Rombold and all the other calves out to live permanently in the fields in April or May.

And now all that steady background was in ruins and he had to start drawing altogether different pictures in his mind. It was a painful business. He sat there for a long time, so long that the two calves got so accustomed to his presence that they stopped nosing and licking him and just lay down beside him.

In the end he reached a fairly comforting conclusion, which he even stated in actual words to the calves, knowing that no one else would be able to hear him because all the buildings were humming with the noise of the milking operations.

'It will be all right so long as I can hang on to Temba and Kirsty.'

10

Temba Dawn from Inside

One morning in October he woke very early with a lot
to think about. It was the Thursday before the mid-
term holiday. He was going to have this day off school
as well as the week-end, for two reasons. One was, so
that he could drive in early with his mother to Aberdeen
docks to meet Kirsty and her mother who were arriving
from Kirkwall. The other was, so that he could help
with the preparations for tomorrow. Tomorrow was the
day of the sale, the fatal day for Tomallen Farm, the
day when it would finally cease to be a farm at all. With
one exception, every movable and valuable thing on the
farm, alive or dead, was going to be sold. It was awful,
lying in bed thinking about it, but yet it was rather exciting too, because of all the weeks of hard work that
had been done to get everything ready and looking its
best. With one exception, everything on the farm would
tomorrow be exposed to view, exposed to hundreds of
prying eyes, and would then have its price called out by
the big voice of the auctioneer and nailed down solid
with the blow of his hammer. The sadness of it all was
covered over by the excitement, but it was there, nag-
ging away underneath. It was like having a moderate
tummy-ache at a party. You knew it was there and that
it might start giving you hell at any moment, but you
hoped for the best and smiled all you could.

He got up as soon as strong daylight came, which was about seven o'clock. He found his mother dressing, but his father was already out in the yards. Lately he had been going out every morning about six.

'Breakfast when we come back,' said his mother briskly, and off they went to the docks through a misty autumn morning that was promising a sunny day later. It had been a very golden autumn. It was the 19th of October and there had been hardly any frosts yet. The little gardens in front of the town houses still had their roses and dahlias in bloom.

The first thing Kirsty said when she had run down the gangplank off the ship was,

'Oh, you look older, Rob! Doesn't he look a lot older, Mum?'

'So do you look older, Kirsty. Oh, I . . . uh . . ,' Rob stammered.

'What's the matter?' she flashed him a big smile. 'I'm glad. Aren't you?'

'Yes, I am. You look great, Kirsty, just great!'

'Well, you look fine, Kirsty—just fine!'

Her face was certainly glowing with excitement. She was on top of the world because one of her paintings had won a prize in a children's art competition. That was one reason why her mother was bringing her on this visit, so that she could see her painting exhibited at the Arts Centre in Aberdeen. Rob had heard about that, of course, but had forgotten and only now, when he saw her face, realised how much it meant to her.

But his mother had not forgotten. As soon as the luggage was loaded into the landrover, she politely brought the subject up, so all the important happenings at the farm had to wait until they were nearly home. Rob sat next to Kirsty in the back, saying nothing at first, listening to her but feeling 'out of it' because she used special terms in talking about painting and drawing. She had become quite an artist, it seemed, full of plans for being one professionally when she grew up.

At breakfast he could tell that she hadn't given a thought to what was happening at the farm. He noticed how her face changed as the reality of it worked its way into her mind.

His father at the end of the table was eating his breakfast while at the same time trying to cope with business letters and herd-books and milk-record sheets and all kinds of forms that needed to be filled in before the sale tomorrow. He was so harassed he was almost steaming. He couldn't spare more than a few absent-minded words for the visitors. Rob could tell from his behaviour to them that he did not want them there at all. It was probably his mother then, Rob suddenly realised, who had invited them to come just at this time —and that could be because—yes, of course, why hadn't he thought of it before—she had quite likely done it for *him*, Rob, so that Kirsty could take his mind off the grief of seeing all the animals sold.

While Rob's mother was explaining some of the difficulties of the sale to Kirsty's mother, he could watch Kirsty begin trying to see it all from his point of view.

'Oh, but what about your Temba Dawn?' she asked in sudden keen interest, which was just what he had been waiting for. He felt free to talk at last. He hurried to explain how Temba was already safely tucked away in an old shed behind the hay barns where no one would see her.

'And anyway I've put a notice outside that says NOT FOR SALE and I've got a padlock to put on the door tomorrow. But I'm going to take her out today to say goodbye to Rombold.'

'Oh yes—Rombold,' Kirsty said thoughtfully. 'I suppose he's quite big now—and then there's—'

'Rombold's *enormous*,' said Rob. 'He's got his ring in his nose. He's a real proper bull already and he's been allowed to serve some heifers. He's had a go on Temba Dawn and John thinks—'

Suddenly he broke off, feeling Kirsty's mother's eyes on him. She had started listening and was going a little red in the face. He remembered that she was an artist, she knew an awful lot about painting and drawing, she always wore beautiful clothes and he couldn't imagine her clumping about the yards in rubber boots to get to know the cows. So with a bit of a wink at Kirsty he dropped that subject and switched on to telling how he was going to be allowed to take Rombold into the salering tomorrow and lead him round, all by himself.

After breakfast, as soon as Kirsty and her mother had done some unpacking in the guest-room, Rob took Kirsty out on to the farm.

'You'll just be an ordinary boy, won't you, when the farm's sold.'

Rob halted in his tracks in sheer surprise. She was looking at him sideways, eyes narrowed into long slits because they had just walked out from behind the house into the full glow of the slanting October sunshine. Her eyes, and indeed her whole face, had that special teasing glint that he always remembered first when thinking of her.

'Oh no, I won't, because I've got Temba—and I'm going to keep her *whatever* happens.'

They just stared at each other, not hostile, but in a kind of deep struggle that he was determined to win. For the first time it occurred to him that she might be jealous of his farm and his Temba. Perhaps she had been, all along, in secret, and now she was letting it show. She was really a bit above herself because of her picture in the exhibition. Oh well, what a good thing she also had something special.

'Come on!' He suddenly seized her hand, rather masterfully. 'We'll go and see Temba first, she's been in that horrible old shed all night by herself and I bet she's awfully bored and miserable.'

All the buildings were full of noisy activity. The farmer had taken on two extra men and was there himself directing operations. That meant four strong men working all-out on a job that had to be finished before noon next day. The whole steading vibrated with feverish energy. All the animals on the farm had to be brushed and polished, all the implements and machines and tools on the farm had to be cleaned up and taken out to be displayed in rows in the nearest field, all the byres and yards had to be washed over and provided with fresh straw. The farm's two tractors were coming and going incessantly, most of the cows and heifers were indoors when they should normally be out quietly grazing. Bales of the very best hay were being broken open and distributed to all the mangers.

The children skirted round all this turmoil on their way to Temba Dawn's shed. Rob had found it best lately not to let himself be seen unless he were ready for some hard scrubbing work. But at one point, where the smell of hay floating out became especially noticeable, he made a quick foray into one of the smaller byres and came back with an armful of it, which he held out towards Kirsty's face.

'Just smell that!'

Because he had already pushed his own nose into it, he was having a flashback in time to the summer evening when this hay had been baled. He had been helping in the field when his father, on the big tractor with the baler behind, had come roaring down along the last row of hay and stopped beside him. It was half past ten, with dew beginning to take the rustle out of the hay. His father had turned off his engine, jumped down from his seat and gone behind the baler to read the number. Then he had pressed his nose into the last bale, still on the baler, and said to Rob in the lovely silence that had gathered, 'Smell that, son, and don't forget. There's no finer smell in the world. And then away with ye to bed.'

Now it was Kirsty burying her nose in his little armful and finding it good.

'Better than lavender,' she said. 'We have lots of that in our garden at home and we pick it and make a fuss of it every year, but it gets a bit sickly.'

As soon as he opened the door, there was Temba

Dawn standing just inside, patient, silent, expectant, having waited long hours for just this. It was Rob she wanted, he believed, not the sweet-smelling hay in his hands, though she was pleased enough with that to start coiling it into her mouth without delay.

'Oh my goodness!' Kirsty cried out in amazement. 'She's a cow! She's grown-up!'

Yes, thirteen months now. She was old enough to have plenty of thoughts and feelings. But there was not room enough in that long dark head for much brain, that was what prevented her from developing a language and entering the world of mind, the world of human beings.

'Look,' said Rob, measuring with his finger the distance from her eyes to the top of her skull, when her long black nose was raised so as to be parallel with the floor. 'You see, there's only about an inch and it's mostly solid bone. Feel here.'

Kirsty smoothed a hand over one of Temba's eyebrows and then across the hard level flatness of her forehead.

'It's the same with all animals,' Rob continued. 'Dad showed me that last time we went to the zoo. They don't have any tops to their heads, even the chimps don't. Turn your head sideways, Kirsty.'

He put a finger-tip on Kirsty's forehead, where it met the bridge of her nose, and ran it lightly up through her hair to the top of her head. Her skin was silky and his finger enjoyed it, but he had more important things in mind.

'There, you see—it's about four inches—and it'll be

86

more still when you're grown-up. And it's all brains in there, four inches of brains.'

Kirsty was looking very thoughtful. 'Let's see yours then. Turn your head over that way.'

She ran her finger gravely up his brow. 'Yes, I see what you mean. It goes straight up. So the poor animals are all hopelessly low-brow creatures. It's a bit unfair on them, isn't it?'

'Yes, it is. If they had brains they'd never let us do the things we do to them. They wouldn't even like us, p'rhaps.'

'Oh, I think they would,' Kirsty said quickly. 'If we really liked them. They'd know, of course. Well, they know even now, don't they, without brains. You *love* Temba, Rob, don't you, so she would love you back even if she did have brains, she might even love you more.'

Rob slipped an arm round the heifer's neck and leaned on her while she munched through the hay. She was the right height for leaning on and she was really solid, you could lean all your weight on her and she wouldn't give way an inch. She might weigh 800 pounds now, his father had said while warning him to be careful in case she put a foot down on one of his.

Yes, she was old enough to have plenty of thoughts and feelings. Did she *really* care for him? He would probably never know for certain. Obviously what she most cared about now was that thing inside her, that bit of Rombold that even now, while she munched, she was slowly but busily turning into a calf.

He leaned over and looked intently into her eyes.

87

'It's funny, she's never looked like this before.'

Kirsty came closer. 'Like what?'

'Her eyes are different. They've gone worried. Yes, that's what it is, she's got scared and worried by being alone. Dad says they all hate it. Oh well, I'll just have to come and be with her more.'

As soon as Temba had finished the hay, Rob slipped her halter on.

'Open the door, Kirsty—we'll take her out to see Rombold. For the last time.'

The moment the door opened Temba became very excited and charged out through it so quickly that Rob almost let go of the rope. He had to run beside her, struggling to prevent her from taking off at the gallop. She seemed to know which way to go.

'I think Rombold's in the nursery field,' said Rob, as they skirted the buildings once more, both tugging back on the rope. 'He was yesterday, with two dry cows who are rather snooty with him.'

They heard his voice before they reached the gate. He must have either seen them or smelled them, for he was waiting for them with his nose up against its bars. Kirsty hung back nervously as Rob opened it, for Rombold snorted with excitement and he was big for his fifteen months.

'He's as tame as a pony, Kirsty, really he is. You must shut the gate after us. Come on.'

He led Temba through and the bull and the heifer at once began licking each other's face.

'There, you see. That's what they do instead of talking.'

88

Kirsty watched Rombold intently, fascinated by the muscles that rippled under the shiny black pelt. He might be young, almost a child compared with Dewarch, but already there was something about his neck and shoulders that inspired awe.

'He's still noble,' she said, 'but I think he's rather awful—I mean, *too* strong.'

After a few minutes, Rob said—

'Isn't it horrible, she'll probably never see a bull again in all her life.'

Kirsty stared. 'Why ever not?'

'Because there aren't any bulls except on the big farms. The crofters have to have A.I. You just ring up and a chap comes out in a car with the stuff and puts it in your cows. That's what we'll have to do with Temba next time, Dad says.'

Nightmare Day

It was a bad morning for Rob. He could not recognise the farm any more. There were strange loud-voiced men going about all over the place, working out the routine for the auction. The sale was to start at twelve o'clock, with the tools and implements and machinery, and everyone but himself seemed to be frantically busy. He might as well not have had any parents, for they were at their wits' end from the start of the day. As for Kirsty, some relations had come in a car and taken her and her mother off into Aberdeen for the whole morning. So he was left on his own.

His father had given him the job of grooming the calves and younger heifers, but his heart was not in the job. When the loose-box where he was working was invaded by a couple of tough men who came to paste lot-numbers on each calf's rump, Rob retired from the scene. He didn't like the impatient way they handled the calves. Besides, Temba was blaring. He knew her voice so well now that he could have picked it out from a thousand cow-voices.

It was just before the sale began that he crossed the stackyard to her shed, the only part of the farm that still felt like home. It was his fourth visit to her that morning and he intended it to be a long one. He would sit down inside her shed with her and let the death of the farm begin without him.

As he neared her shed he heard strange bumping noises and when he reached the door he saw it bulging and heaving against its hinges and its padlock.

'Temba!' he called sharply. 'Temba, don't! Stop it!'

He put his face close to the gap along the top of the door and discovered her eyes there, very close and big and wide and frightened. She must have been shoving with all her weight against the door, for she was still panting with the exertion.

But she gave him a moo of welcome as he undid the padlock and she did not try to push past him when he opened the door. He slipped quickly inside, shut it behind him, then ran his hands down along her neck and under her chin, talking to her all the while.

'I know—I know you're all upset—I know what it feels like. It's all right, it's all right, Temba—I know the farm's gone mad today, but it'll be all over soon, quite soon now—and then I'll take you out for a walk this evening when it's all over.'

She listened, of course. He could watch her ears twist and turn as she took in the caressing tones of his voice. But she was listening also to that threatening hubbub from the steading, which was plainly giving her the horrors. She was sniffing, too—but not at him. She was holding her nose to the gap over the door and wrinkling it disgustedly and then wiping inside her nostrils with her tongue. She was obviously telling him, 'There's something horribly wrong with the farm today, and what's more it stinks to high heaven. I can't stand much more of this, it's getting me down.'

Rob could feel it too—not smell it, but feel it as well as hear it. The auction must be just about starting now. From over there beyond the haystacks something came floating on currents of air right into this shed, right into his and Temba's nerves. It was something that was getting under their skins, something hostile to everything warm and living and beautiful.

Temba lifted her nose, hollowed her back and let forth what was probably the loudest blare she had made in her life. It went out so powerfully that Rob knew she was bound to get some answers. In fact she got three at least, all of which she could probably recognise. Rob could only distinguish one and that was Rombold's, for he had the specially high-pitched voice that is usual in young bulls.

Rob stayed on and on with Temba, listening to the auctioneer's voice that had now begun to penetrate all over the farm. He forgot all about dinner (which he would not have been able to eat in any case). He wanted only to pass the time away until late afternoon when he would have to do his important job with Rombold. He had promised his father to do that and he knew it was a great honour. However much he dreaded it, he knew there was no possibility of escape. Rombold was the prize animal at Tomallen, his father had several times explained to him. It mattered extremely how Rombold behaved in the sale-ring and this would depend partly upon *him*, Rob. It made him go weak at the knees even to think of it. Rombold would be the last to be sold, after the calves and the heifers and the cows, except for Dewarch who would be the last of all.

At last Rob started tearing himself away. A chorus of anxious mooings and blarings had begun over there beyond the haystacks, from which he could tell that the selling of the livestock was well under way. Dewarch's great voice, which Rob knew almost as well as Temba's, had begun to dominate the farm. As he let himself out of Temba's shed, Rob heard a very loud blare from Dewarch that for the first time had an unmistakable note of anger in it. What on earth would happen, he wondered, if Dewarch really went on the war-path now. If Temba, sweet-tempered Temba, felt so bad about the situation, how awfully bad might not the lordly Dewarch feel, suspecting that his herd of wives and daughters were being bullied about by a crowd of strange shouting men?

Just in time, Rob remembered that he must do something about Temba's door. After thinking for a minute and examining its hinges and its fastening, he went over to one of the stacks and picked up a stout pole that was lying alongside it. Bringing it back to the shed he planted it firmly against the door as a prop, then went off towards the steading feeling just that much the better for a sensible bit of work.

The next thing was to find Kirsty, for she had promised to help him with Rombold. He discovered her waiting about anxiously for him in the house and together they hurried straight to the young bull's loose-box. There was no time to talk. He just gave her orders. For the next half-hour, while he was giving Rombold a final grooming and washing, she ran backwards and forwards between him and the sale-ring so as to keep

93

him informed on how many cows there were left, before Rombold's turn came. She could give him also a rough idea of how the cows were selling, for she could see the faces of the farmer and of John as they controlled each one inside the ring. She said they both looked well enough pleased, though harassed.

As the moment approached when he would have to lead Rombold down the passage and through the gate into the big yard, Rob felt his heart hammering so hard inside his chest that he almost began to fear *that* more than anything else. It was a worse hammering than he had had after trying to win the 100 yards sprint in the school sports. Supposing something gave way inside his body?

He was not in the least scared or even worried about Rombold's behaviour in the ring, as he knew his father and John both were about Dewarch's. Rombold's nose-ring, recently put in, had made it impossible for him to assert his bull-will, even in play. Rob had only to put one finger through his ring and he became as submissive as a well-trained dog. That was either because his nose was still very sensitive or because he was an unusually good-tempered creature, or perhaps a little of both. 'He's had a happy childhood,' the farmer often said, 'that's the secret of it. God knows what sort of childhood Dewarch had.'

What was making Rob's heart hammer so badly was the crowd, the noisy, shouting, smoking, joking, smelly, inquisitive crowd. He had seen enough of it during the morning to last him a long time. He had seen its greedy fingers poking into everything, even into the cows' mouths, seen its eyes, full of suspicion and craftiness, peering and probing into and under and behind everything. He had suddenly realised that, as soon as he entered the ring with Rombold, not only the bull but he also, *he*, the farmer's boy, the special person on Tomallen Farm, would be under inspection by the crowd. That was the terrifying thought, all the more so because it was new. He had actually *asked* to do this terrifying thing, to be allowed to lead Rombold into the ring and round it all by himself. That was because he had never really looked at the crowd at close quarters, he had seen it casually in markets or at football matches but had never *inspected* it in the way it was going to inspect him.

But having asked to do this he knew he would just have to go through with it, there was no possible escape. The arrangements were all made. His father and John were completely up to their necks in the sale, completely out of his reach. There was no one else to do it.

Kirsty was coming through the door.

'It's time, Rob. John says, bring him down the passage now and wait at the gate. Oh goodness, Rob, you do look white!'

But it was all right. As soon as he had something to do, the internal hammering died away.

'Come down the passage with me, Kirsty,' he said, untying Rombold's rope. In moments like this it never occurred to him that he was giving orders rather than making requests.

It was only a short wait for him and Rombold at the gate, but it was long enough for every face in the crowd

95

to turn and look at what was waiting, for they could be plainly seen through the bars of the gate. Rob felt all those faces and eyes spraying over him like fierce rays of light. He and Rombold were coming into the ring from a different direction from the one used by the heifers and cows. For the crowd, this was something new and special which had been kept till nearly the end. It was an entertainment now as well as a sale.

The auctioneer intended to make the most of it. But as Rob entered the ring, with Rombold prancing grandly beside him, he was in such a state of tension that he only heard a quarter of what the man was saying.

'Now, *there's* a sight for sore eyes!' shouted the big voice. 'As fine a young bull as I've ever seen in my life— and I've seen more than most—and there he is in the hands of an eleven-year-old boy—look at that now—as docile as a lamb, but already in use as a stud bull.

'Who'll give me five hundred guineas?'

It was by far the best thing that happened that day, so everyone said afterwards. It was so good that it was able to overshadow the bad thing that came later. Rombold made a price well above all expectations. There were so many farmers there who had been deciding, reluctantly, to use artificial insemination for their cows, although they much preferred to use a bull if only they could find one easy enough to handle. Rombold was exactly what they wanted.

Rob had to stay in the ring leading Rombold round and round for a good ten minutes. As it was the next-to-last item in the sale, the auctioneer was no longer in a hurry. He stuck to his starting figure of five hundred guineas until someone at last offered it and then he ran it up to five hundred and sixty-five, double what the farmer had hoped for. When the hammer fell and Rob led Rombold out, there was a vigorous round of hand-clapping, which was very unusual at a farm sale.

Taking Rombold down the passage again, with Kirsty dancing beside him, Rob was walking on air. As soon as he had tied up the young bull safely in the loose-box, he wanted to hurry off to find his father and talk about the wonderful price and get praised for his part in it. But that was not to be—not yet, for there was something else to be got through first.

His father and John, and the two other men who were helping, were all busy bringing Dewarch Prince into the ring and they were having trouble. The big bull was roaring. All day he had been calling out in a high-pitched protesting voice, but now for the first time he was making very deep angry roars. They domi-nated the entire farm.

There was a five-minute period of shouts and warn-ing cries and pushing and scrambling amongst the crowd. Some of them were trying to get away from the ring because they feared there might be trouble, some of them were trying to get closer to it because they hoped there would be and were determined to have a good view of it. Rob and Kirsty, being on the outskirts of all this, climbed up on to the third bar of one of the closed gates on the far side of the yard and so had a good vantage point.

Dewarch came into the ring at last, at the run, with the farmer running on one side of him and John on the other, each of them holding him by a bull-stick hitched to his nose-ring. They brought him to a halt, with difficulty, and for half a minute he stood there roaring and pawing the ground. First with one front hoof, then with the other, he scooped up wodges of damp straw and showered them over his back and shoulders.

The auctioneer ought to have been calling out the bull's name and number and record, but he was not, he was only watching.

Suddenly he shouted out very loud, 'Take him back. We'll sell him in his stall.'

But just as he was shouting that out, Dewarch went down on his knees, dug his huge head into the ground and gave a sideways roll which snatched the two bull-sticks out of the men's hands as if they were match-sticks. The sticks went down underneath him, one of them took his entire weight and crumpled. He let out a great bellow of anger and pain, rolled fully over and then scrambled to his feet with blood coming from his nose.

Several men were shouting. 'His ring's out!' 'He's pulled his ring out!'

The farmer and John had dived for the sticks and now held them once more, but all they had at their ends was a ring, not a bull.

There was panic in parts of the crowd, there was a surge of people to the exits from the yard.

Rob and Kirsty had to fly for their lives, their gate was seized and flung open by a mob of people who were half laughing and half swearing, trying to hide their fear. But in the distance Rob heard his father's voice, calling out, very loud indeed and as steady as a rock,

'Open all the gates and let him *go*!'

He did go, at a lurching trot, still roaring and swinging his tail like mad. Rob had a last glimpse of his father and John going off after him. All three of them disappeared into the distance, while the auctioneer was announcing at the top of his voice that Dewarch Prince must be withdrawn from the sale and that the day's business was over.

Clinging tight to one of Kirsty's hands, Rob scuttled down a dark passage into the granary and undid an old door which let them both through into the stackyard away from all the upheaval and commotion. He hardly knew what he was doing, he was in a blind panic, he only wanted to escape. He shut the door behind them and leaned back against it, gasping for breath. All those excited people, all that shouting—it was just too much. It had got him down at last. Tomallen Farm had turned into a nightmare. His legs felt peculiar, they were folding under him, he was slipping down, down, Kirsty's staring face above him was fading away into a mist.

'Rob! Rob! Whatever's the matter—wake up— Rob, *please*!'

She was pulling at him, shaking him almost, as he lay on the ground. Then suddenly it was all right, the mist cleared, he could see her face properly and behind her the solid comfortable wall of one of the big haystacks. He scrambled to his feet, testing his legs, putting his hands behind him to feel the rough granite blocks of

99

the granary wall.

'Come on, Kirsty!' He grabbed her hand again and they hurried on together through the stackyard towards Temba's shed. It was all he could think of just then, to go and be with Temba, to take refuge in the one corner of the farm that still belonged to him, that still made sense.

Rounding the corner of another big stack of bales, they had Temba's shed in full view in front of them. Its door lay splintered on the ground and it was empty.

I 2

Telephone the Butcher!

His father woke him at dawn, as he had promised. Rob sprang out of bed instantly, scrambled into his clothes and ran down to the kitchen. His father was there making tea. He looked bleary-eyed and older than usual as he turned to take a good look at his son.

'So you *did* sleep, Rob! I had to shake you awake.'

'Yes—but I dreamed Temba was dead. She was just a great black heap lying by the side of a road. Did *you* sleep, Dad?'

'Och yes. But I took some pills to help me. It's a pity we didn't give something of the kind to that bull—maybe that's the one bad mistake I've made over this sale.'

'Oh. D'you mean—would that have put him in a good temper?'

'I could have got the vet to give him the right sort of injection. There's a good chance that would have stopped him from getting wild. Only it would have been hard on the man who bought him.'

The farmer sipped his second cup of tea, then added,

'Maybe I'm glad I didn't. I wouldn't want the last thing I did as a farmer to spoil my reputation as an honest man, would I?'

Rob thought it over, then went to the window to peer out.

'There's quite a lot of light—as much as there was that morning Temba was born. Can we go now?'

'In a minute, Rob. Don't hurry me. I'm about as tired as I've ever been in my life, besides being worried.'

'Where shall we go first, Dad?'

'I've got it worked out, roughly. They'll be together, I reckon. Dewarch had a good hour of daylight left, time enough to get a good feed of grass *and* find himself some company if there was any to find. We can guess your heifer broke out earlier in the afternoon. So they'll be together where the best grass is, most likely. And that's the Ten Acre, where there's a water trough too.'

It was so like the morning of Temba's birth that as soon as they were out under the sky Rob began to feel the burden of anxiety lifting. Some of the stars were still shining, but the sky over towards the sea was a miracle of gold and green.

The farm was strangely silent. Even the poultry were gone, no cock could crow. There was not a single animal left in the whole steading except a cat or two, perhaps, unless either Temba or Dewarch had come back indoors during the night, which the farmer said was highly improbable.

After they had collected Temba's halter from her shed and Rob had just said, 'You'll need one for Dewarch, Dad, won't you?' his father replied,

'No, son, I'm afraid no one's ever going to put a halter on Dewarch again, not single-handed anyway. The risks are too great. Without a nose-ring it's pretty near impossible to put him under safe control.'

Rob thought about that in silence as they made their

102

way towards the Ten Acre. When they neared its gate, which stood open, he ran ahead and started to climb up on to its post to get a wide view. But there was no need for even as he climbed he saw the two black shapes in the distance, one twice the size of the other. They were grazing, side by side. His heart began to pound.

His father came up and said in a low voice,

'Now, do *exactly* what I tell you, Rob, and don't talk. Do you understand?'

Rob nodded.

'Walk slowly behind me,' continued the farmer, 'and when we reach your heifer slip her halter on and bring her slowly back towards the gate. If she comes to meet us, so much the better.'

She did come to meet them. She pushed her nose right into Rob's chest, making it easy for him to halter her and get her on the move. Not until she was following him readily across the field did he glance at the bull, who simply stood watching.

'Carry on,' said the farmer, coming along behind. 'But keep it slow.'

They reached the gate and still Dewarch only stood there staring. 'Take her through,' said the farmer, still watching the bull.

Then he came through himself and took Temba's halter rope from his son. 'Now, you go home, Rob, at a steady pace, and I'll come after you with Temba as soon as Dewarch starts to follow. Do you understand? With any luck he'll follow her right back into his own house. But I want you *out of the way* when we reach the steading.'

'Okay, Dad.'

He made his steady walk a fairly brisk one, twisting his head back over a shoulder most of the time. He was half way through the next field when he saw his father and Temba start away from the gate. A few moments later he saw Dewarch's great bulk come through the gateway, in a slow ambling way as if he were just mildly interested.

When Rob reached the steading he climbed a high yard gate and then on to the roof of a shed. From there he could watch the great bull come steadily on behind Temba and his father, across the first yard, into the buildings, and then disappear down the passage in the direction of his bull-house. Obviously he was thinking more of his breakfast than of anything else. His nose looked torn, but there was no blood showing on it. He would have cleaned it up thoroughly with his tongue.

Rob's father came to fetch him, smiling with relief.

'All's well. We can go in now and see if there's any breakfast ready for us. Temba's in Rombold's box and Dewarch's eating hay, as quiet as an old cow.'

But just then John arrived, coming across the fields from his house, so the situation had to be explained to him. Rob listened intently while the two men talked.

At the end of it the farmer announced, making his words tell,

'I'm taking no risks, John, and I'm not having you take any either.'

John shook his head sadly. 'As good as dead, then, that's what the poor bugger is. Ah weel, I'm nae surprised. He'll die respected. There's some that'll never give up. You can kill 'em, but you canna master 'em.'

Going in to breakfast, Rob tried to get more information from his father, but found it difficult.

'Well, you see, son, what I have to do now is, get on the telephone to a butcher I know. If he's interested I can do a deal with him. If he isn't, some other butcher will be. There's many hundred-weights of good meat on that bull. I wouldn't mind giving it away, but I'll not have it wasted.'

'But how's he going to be killed, Dad? And when?'

'That's something I'm hoping to leave to the experts. They'll get him away from here alive if they can, but it'll be their responsibility, not mine. And now you've got to stop thinking about him, son. He's had a happy life since he came here and we've always done the best we can for him. But it's *over*, see? And that's all there is to it.'

Rob said nothing. He wasn't crying, but he saw his father's quick glance at his face in case he might be. Really he was searching for something to say, something that would be fairly grown-up and serve to hide his feelings.

Since he found nothing, his father continued as they entered the farmhouse,

'You've got your Temba—and a good thing too. Without her, I doubt if we would ever have got him home. We might have had to go after him with guns.'

13
A Change of Scene

Later that morning he and Kirsty and their mothers
drove into Aberdeen to see Kirsty's picture. In the big
rooms at the Arts Centre, with their walls covered by
things hatched out of the imaginations of hundreds of
children, Rob felt a stranger. Here was another world
altogether, but one which Kirsty's face told him was
very important, not only to her but in its own right.

They had to find her picture first, of course. It was
one of those marked with a red star to show that it was a
prize-winner. What impressed Rob was not so much the
picture itself, which was of a little house with huge
trees growing round and over it, but the dreamy way
she stood looking at it as if she were the only person in
the room. She was alone with it in that milling crowd
with two grown-ups and a boy intently watching her to
see what she felt about it. When he and his mother said
nice things over it, she just gave them a silent look.
Almost, she looked through them.

Kirsty had to see the whole exhibition and as they
moved slowly through it Rob felt more and more
peculiar. His own farm-world having come to bits,
he was trying to take a new look at life without it, so he
was unusually free in his mind, sort of floating in space.
And at this very moment he was being faced with all
these pictures, so very alive and warm and flashing in

every possible colour and shape. They were like little doors, secret doors, each one as you looked at it suddenly opening to show you a fleeting glimpse of someone else's private magic country where you didn't belong.

He gaped and wondered and kept on looking at Kirsty in the hope of seeing as much as she was seeing. He only looked once at her mother, in spite of knowing that she was an artist, because her face was screwed up, not wide open and absorbing like Kirsty's.

On their way back to the farm about dinner-time, when they were already on the Tomallen private road, Rob's mother had to pull the landrover on to the grass and stop, because a cattle-lorry was approaching them.

As it went by, Rob was straining his ears. Yes, he could just hear something big and alive in there. He met his mother's glance, but said nothing, nor did she, not even when Kirsty, after taking her time over it, suddenly guessed.

'Oh, Rob, could that be Dewarch in there—going?'

Still no one said anything and no one, not even Rob, asked his father about it when they reached the house. The farmer had such a very distant face and he kept looking out of the windows as if he wanted to escape.

At dinner he said, bursting out with it, his voice over-flowing with something,

'Let's go to the mountains. I never needed a change of scene so much in all my life.'

He drove fast on the lonely road past the Hill of Fare, then to Ballater and from there out on the mountain road to Loch Muick. There were hardly any cars on the road in spite of golden weather, for it was too late in the season. He turned into a lay-by and switched off his engine.

'Listen!' He held up a hand just in time to stop anyone from speaking.

Stag-voices were drifting down from the high hills. Similar to cattle-voices but wilder, rather like a mixture of cows blaring and donkeys braying, and coming from every point of the compass. The entire hill-country had an undulating blanket of sound lying upon it as naturally as mist or snow.

Kirsty and her mother had not heard it before. Rob and his father explained about October being the rutting season for the red deer and said they had a good chance of seeing some of them if they could approach them down-wind. They left the landrover and set off into the wilds.

The wind being north, the farmer took them across the river Muick and then up into some high corries on Conacraig mountain. They saw deer many times, mostly small bunches of hinds being chivvied about by loudly belling stags. But they were not able to keep quiet enough to get really close. Kirsty got so excited that every time she caught sight of a stag she had to call out, 'Oh, look—look!' which meant that all the deer in the neighbourhood took fright.

As they crouched together behind a rock, up to their shoulders in heather, peering for glimpses of tawny bodies, she whispered to Rob, 'Oh, wouldn't it be lovely to be *wild*, absolutely wild, and go skimming over rocks like that, hardly touching, not thinking, just flying and dreaming—'

He whispered back, 'But not for always—it would get *boring*.'

On the way home, during a silence as they sped along in the dusk, Kirsty asked,

'What are they making all that noise *about*, really?'

The women and children waited for the farmer to answer. They all felt, with those haunting stag-voices still sounding in their ears, that any answer would need to have some trouble taken over it.

'Well, Kirsty, you'd need to be a red deer yourself to find that out. But I can guess it's the long highland summer in 'em, all those endless-daylight days on the high hills—and then all those endless miles of heather flowering round 'em, drunk on heather they could be. In winter they skulk in the glens, but all summer they're away up there free as the wind, lording it—it's the pride in them, boiling over, telling the world, that's what it is.

'They've never been tamed, never had rings through their noses.'

It was dark by the time they reached home. Not telling even Kirsty, Rob slipped out at once to see Temba, thinking of all the other times when they had come back after dark from a family outing. On all the other times that he could remember it had been his father who had hurried out at once to see if everything was all right in the steading and on the farm. But tonight his father had gone into the sitting-room and switched on the television.

Rob wanted to make it up to Temba for leaving her alone all day. Since shutting her into Rombold's box in the early morning he had done nothing for her, not even brought her any hay. He also wanted to compare her shape with that of the many hinds they had seen in the mountains. With their flowing, leaping movements still vivid in his mind, he had to admit that Temba was decidedly over-solid. Perhaps he was over-feeding her.

When he had finished grooming and petting her he went down the passage to the bull's house, switching on lights as he went. Its door stood open, emptiness and silence reigned there already. There was no sign of any struggle having taken place.

He entered, feeling a need to set foot in what had always been forbidden ground. In the corner by the iron bars something scrabbled and fled over the side of the manger, too quick for his eyes to follow. He stood motionless with fright, then saw some cubes of cow-cake in the manger and knew a rat must have been eating there. That, probably, was the remains of Dewarch's last meal, or the bait which men had used to capture him that morning and lead him out to the lorry.

Rob stood for a while looking out through those massive iron bars into the passage where he had stood so many times looking in, trying to read Dewarch's thoughts. He was at it again now. Here Dewarch must have stood eating his last rackful of hay, thinking of his cows, wondering where they could all have gone. Well, at least he would have had some conversation with Temba. She would have heard him go and been able to call goodbye. And she would not have known that he was going to his death.

14

Moving House

For the next few weeks, while his parents were hunting for another home, Rob had to get accustomed to living in a dead farm. It was hard, but he knew it was equally hard for Temba and his father, so that made it easier to bear.

It was the darkest time of the year, too. On school days he could not even take Temba out for walks. He could only visit her with a torch (the electricity in the steading had been turned off) before breakfast and after school, to make sure that she had plenty of food and water and dry bedding. At first she used her voice a lot, especially in the early mornings. Often when he was on his way out to her before breakfast he would hear her lonely bellows echoing all through the big empty spaces of the steading, down long passages into empty byres and empty barns, then fading away across empty yards and fields. Since she never received any answers, it wasn't long before she gave up bellowing altogether.

She was living in the stone-built loose-box right in the heart of the buildings, the one she had once shared with Rombold in the long-ago days of her happy child-hood. (They seemed to Rob to be long-ago days now, because she was so big and growing bigger all the time.) It had been Rombold's special loose-box for a few weeks before the sale. Rob thought it probable, and hoped so for Temba's sake, that it still had the smell of the young bull hanging about in it. Its door was solid oak, with a thick iron bar to close it. He never saw Temba even think of trying to break out of there. She must have known there was no point in it, since there was only silence and emptiness throughout the farm.

At the week-ends, when he had given her a good long walk in the morning, he got into the habit of spending whole afternoons sitting beside her on his milking-stool reading a book. She would lie there chewing her cud and he would read. It seemed a fair exchange of companionship, except that sometimes, after she had got through a whole armful of cabbage that he had brought her from the garden, she would belch up such a strong gas round him that it made all his senses reel for a minute.

He often read out loud because it was fun to see her ears twitching every now and then as his voice rose and sank over the conversational bits. To read a book out there well away from the house, out of reach of interruptions like human voices or the telephone and radio, somehow made a story come right off the pages and run away with him. *Warrior Scarlet* was one of the books that he read out there and he was pretty sure it was going to stay with him for the rest of his life.

He became so keen on reading that he did not invite his school friends out to the farm any more. When his parents urged him to do so, he said, 'It isn't really much good now the farm's gone dead. They might soon get bored, you see, now there's only Temba.'

It was early December before the great day came

113

when his parents took him to see the house they had decided to buy. He sat between them in the front seat of the landrover for a long drive into the hill-country of Aberdeenshire, with four inches of snow on the roads and hardly any traffic. It was their fourth visit to the place, but his first. His tour of inspection inside lasted only a quarter of an hour, just long enough to give him an impression of a solid ancient grey-granite house, with lots of rooms and views from the windows of distant mountains covered in snow. Then he was outside exploring a wild overgrown garden and a four-acre field with a stone wall round it. There was a shed in the field over on the far side, and just behind the shed, on the other side of the wall, was the edge of a big fir plantation that his father said belonged to the Forestry Commission. It would shelter their new property from the north-east wind. All of this would do fine for Temba, his father kept telling him. The shed had a manger inside and a good roof fitted with a gutter that drained into a water-butt.

After his father had returned to the house, Rob had a long look at everything all over again, storing the impressions that really mattered. The wind from the mountains was moaning quietly in the tops of the fir trees behind the shed. They were big trees, it was a real forest, almost dark inside in spite of the snow. He walked out into the field and back again, making a snow-track that stood out starkly on its smooth white surface as if he had written his signature on it. Then he stood for a while by the open door of the shed, wondering what it would feel like to be lying in there listening to the wind in the forest. He stayed long there, not minding the cold, part of the time even with his eyes shut, just feeling and sensing. There was a long, deep, ancient quietness brooding over the whole place, which he felt he belonged to. A rabbit came out soundlessly from under the wall and gazed at him, wriggling its nose enquiringly—until his mother's voice called him from a window.

That was a Saturday and they moved house about a fortnight later, just before the Christmas holiday started. Luckily for them, the snow had all gone again except in the high hills where it would stay all winter.

A cattle-lorry had to be hired for Temba. It took not only her and all her gear, like halters, feeding-bowls and dung-forks, but also forty bales of best hay and ten bales of straw which the farmer had kept back from his sale especially for her. Rob helped to load the bales and then by his urgent request was allowed to ride in the lorry alongside the driver. There was a little wooden shutter behind their seat which Rob could slide open now and then so that he could look inside at Temba. He would like to have kept it open all the time, but the driver grumbled about the freezing draught it made on their necks.

Driving away in a cattle-lorry was so exciting for Rob that he did not have a single sad thought about never seeing Tomallen again. They must *never* return, his father said, because all they would see next time would be bulldozers and cranes and concrete-mixers. But Rob was hardly happy either. He was too stretched in his nerves for that, because Temba was having a hell of a time just behind him. The farm road was full of pot-holes after all the extra traffic it had taken lately, so the lorry was lurching from side to side as it left the farm. Temba had to scrabble madly with her hooves to keep upright. Rob knew it was a bad thing for in-calf heifers to be thrown to the ground, so he was in a sweat of anxiety. When Temba let out a blare with a note of real terror in it, as if she really thought her last hour was at hand, he implored the driver to slow down. But the man only chuckled, said it would do her no harm to dance a bit, the young ones never went down, and besides he had been told to keep well in sight of the landrover ahead. Rob's parents were driving that, leading the way across country, and behind the lorry came all their household stuff in a furniture van.

At the end of that day, with the sun going down like a crimson ball and the grass already crisp with frost, Rob stood with Temba inside the gate of the four-acre field, talking to her and smoothing her over with his hands, getting ready to take her halter off. She was still trembling a little, but she had her nose down to the pasture already, she seemed to be very interested in it. Now all the snow was gone, the herbage proved to be about five inches long. It might be brown and matted, it was certainly mixed with docks and thistles and nettles, but it hadn't been grazed since the summer. Rob with his farmer's eye could tell that it was going to keep Temba occupied for the rest of the winter, except when it was under snow.

Although he was still smoothing her, she began to move on slowly, tearing and sniffing at the grass. He

116

was still wondering whether it would be safe to take off her halter. After tucking away some fat mouthfuls of grass, she brought her head up and round against his chest, giving him a tiny moo as if to say,

'Try some of this, it's first rate!'

'So you *are* going to like it here Temba,' he said aloud, with enormous relief. 'So am I, I think.'

He was leaning against her to get some of her warmth, for a keen wind had begun sighing in the fir forest. Listening to that, he also heard muffled hammering sounds from inside the house, where his father would be laying the carpets. There was something else coming on the wind, too—something from a distance which had made Temba suddenly go tense all over, with her ears twitching. It was a cow mooing.

That changed his mind about letting her free in the field, even for half an hour while he went to see what was going on in the house. She might get ideas about possible new neighbours. His father had told him that she must certainly be shut into the shed for the first few nights, so he took her in there now, gave her some hay and water and carefully bolted the door on her. Then before going in to his tea he made an inspection all round the field in case there might be weak places where she could push or jump her way out.

Their new house, Craglane, was properly in the country, about ten miles from Aberdeen, standing by itself with its own private road leading to it. Fairly near to it were two farms, one called Crag End, very small, more of a croft than a farm, the other called Crag Mains, a big place with many byres and barns and huge stacks of straw bales. It was easy for Rob to meet the people at Crag Mains because his father went there with him to see about buying some straw for Temba's shed. There was an old man there, with his son and his son's wife and their two babies. At Crag End there were two boys, of nine and eleven, whom Rob met on his third day at his new home. Only it was really they who met him, for they had arranged it beforehand.

He had been out exploring on his bicycle and was nearing home when he had to stop because they were there holding their bicycles broadside-on to make a barrier across the road. He tried to smile at them, in spite of being scared because they looked so tough.

The older one was tall, with long black hair falling over his eyes and a chin that jutted out warningly. He had no gloves, Rob noticed, though it was just about freezing. His hands gripping the bicycle were as knobbly and brown as old potatoes.

'There's a pass-word to give or we won't let you through,' said black-hair curtly, making a thorough inspection of Rob.

'But—I've only just come,' Rob protested. 'How could I know the pass-word?'

He too was having a very good look at them, trying to make out whether they were really hostile or just pretending. He suspected the younger one might be holding his face very tight to prevent a smile.

'I didn't say *the* pass-word,' black-hair said, 'I said *a* pass-word. You've got to think one up or you can't go home.' As the boy said 'home' he glanced at Craglane, so Rob understood that they knew all about him.

'Crag, then,' said Rob at a venture.

Black-hair nodded and moved his bicycle aside. 'Good enough. D'you want to go now?'

'I don't think so,' said Rob. 'There's only me, at home.'

'In that big place? Gee, man, you're lucky.' The boy turned to his brother. 'Shall we show him the hut, Dave?'

Dave the younger one was now all smiles, but black-hair, whose name was Scot, was as tense and serious as before, though no longer hostile. They took Rob back towards Crag End and into a disused quarry, where there were the remains of a tiny shed perched up on a rock-ledge. Its roof let in water and its floor was a pulpy mess of rotten wood, but Rob understood that it meant a lot to them and that showing it to him was an offer of friendship. He was glad to know that he had something to show them in return.

In the new year he had a new school to go to, a real country school with sixty-five children instead of the six hundred that his first school had had. As it was only two miles away he could go by bicycle with Scot and Dave. Many of the children there were sons and daughters of farmers and farm-workers. He would have got on well with them if he had been less reserved and self-sufficient. Except for the headmaster, whom he was not sure about yet, he liked this school better than the other.

Mr Mackay the headmaster was a very devout Bible Christian, the first he had ever met. Rob did not dislike him, but was disturbed inside by him. Nearly every time he spoke, but especially in morning assemblies, Rob got a sinking hollow feeling in the tummy, rather like what happens when you look over the edge of a cliff. He was never boring, which was why Rob could not dislike him. He had a deep resounding voice and greying hair. He was nicknamed 'ole thunder'.

Rob soon discovered that he was mostly bark and hardly any bite. All the same, everyone was scared of him because he seemed to be on such intimate terms with God. They had three assemblies each week, at which he took it for granted that God was present. Besides those, he used to read stories from the Bible to each of the classes on one morning every week, reading them as if he were God's personal assistant. The stories were new to Rob and he was deeply impressed.

Also in the new year his father obtained a job as a cow-cake and fertiliser salesman. It made a surprisingly big difference at Craglane. His mother began to laugh again and found a woman to come and help in the house three days a week. They had nicer food on the table. When Rob came home from school his father would no longer be sitting by the fire reading a newspaper, but would be arriving home himself in a little while, swishing through the gate in his big car, blowing his horn gaily and probably bringing something special for tea that he had picked up in his travels. His job took him all over the country, calling on farmers.

Rob wrote a letter to Kirsty:

Dear Kirsty
    Temba Dawn is all right. I've got a field for her,

and a shed. But she won't go in the shed much, only to eat and drink. I can see the bulge now, where her calf is. My school is quite different. Mr Mackay the headmaster is mad on God and the bible, but I quite like it. I go every day on my bicycle, with two boys from a farm that is quite close. It is a very little farm. My dad has got a job now, so we are happy. I did not know we were not before, but I have found out. I wish you were here. We have a big house far away from anywhere and a big garden. Can you come?

15
Thinking and Reading

One evening in January his father said,

'Those two boys at Crag End, Rob, look like being the only company you'll find here, close to home. You'd better make the most of them. You seem to be turning into rather a bookworm.'

'Yes, Dad, but—'

'Don't you get on with them?'

'Oh, they're okay, but they just fool about all the time. They never think or read a book—and they said Temba's just an ordinary cow.'

'I see, so they bore you. All the same, we would rather have you out with them than sitting in Temba's shed reading all through the week-ends.'

'But I've got such a lot of thinking to do and that's the way I do it. I read out loud and she likes it.'

The farmer and his wife exchanged glances. They knew Rob had taken to reading aloud to Temba and that he had begun it even before they left Tomallen. It had been worrying them for a long time.

'But Rob,' said his mother, 'I can't think how you can keep warm in that flimsy little shed.'

'Temba keeps me warm if I stay close enough to her. And I can put my feet under the straw. I never get bored in there, it's super.'

'What books have you got out there now?' asked his

father.

'Oh—well—one of them's a Bible. I found it in those boxes of books I unpacked when we moved in.'

Rob looked carefully for approval or disapproval in his parents' faces, but saw only surprise. There was that nervous glance flashing between them again, but their silence seemed to mean that they had nothing to say on that subject.

Making an effort, Rob brought out one of his special thoughts.

'Dad, if there *is* a God, do you think he could be farming us, like we do the cows and sheep and everything?'

His father blinked and smiled. 'You know our views, son. Your mother and I are both agnostics, which means we don't know and we don't really—'

His mother broke in. 'If your new school is giving you some new ideas, Rob, that's a very good thing. Mr Mackay may be old-fashioned, but I'm sure he has a heart of gold.'

Rob continued quickly,

'But you see, Mum, he says being happy means letting God use you and not hitting back against him. He says it's like a farm—the animals are happy if they let us use them and don't hit back. We've got power of life and death over them, like God has over us. That means I'm God, to Temba. And Dad was God, to Dewarch.'

His father laughed, got up suddenly from his seat and smacked the fist of one hand into the palm of the other.

'Well, dammit, Rob, you're in deep water—but if

that's where you want to be, and if you can swim there, well, go ahead, that's all I can say. But maybe I'll go and have another chat with this Mr Mackay you're so keen on.'

'I'm not very, Dad, no. He's a bit daft and people laugh at him when he's not there. But he makes you think.'

16
A Midsummer Day

She was lying down at the back of the shed when the children entered. Her head swung slowly to meet them, but she went on cudding and her eyes went on dreaming.

'She comes in here now on all the hot days, to get away from the flies,' he explained. 'But never at night. I keep fly-spray for her here.'

He reached up to a shelf above the window for a spray-gun, pumped it three or four times in Temba's direction, then put it back. Kirsty's eyes fell on the books which were also on the shelf.

'Are those the ones you've been reading aloud to Temba?'

'Yes, they are—but how did you know I've been doing that?'

'It was in a letter from your Mum to mine, especially about the Bible. You *are* an extraordinary boy, Rob. Can I look at it?'

'Help yourself.'

She took down from the shelf a black leather Bible with rice-paper pages, blew dust off it and opened it here and there.

'Oh, Rob, this is terrible—look!'

She showed him a patch on the back cover which had apparently been nibbled. 'It's mice or moths or something. You haven't touched this for ages. I don't believe you've read it at all!'

'I have *so*. Give it me!'

He examined it, looked inside between the back and the binding, then shook out some mice-droppings. 'Yes, it *is* mice. It'll have to go back in the house.'

'How much did you read of it?'

He grinned at her. 'A fair bit, but mainly for the sound, because I couldn't understand it at all. I read some of it when we had March gales and the fir trees were roaring like a mad bull. I had to read very loud and it sounded quite like Mr Mackay. A bit like God too, I should think.'

She stood watching him thoughtfully until he grew suddenly shy, seized a fork and very expertly picked up some recent dung of Temba's and flung it out through the doorway.

'We have the sea to roar, at Kirkwall,' she said, withdrawing her gaze from him at last and looking inwards. 'All the winter it never stops roaring. It's like tigers waiting for you. It was nice, last winter, having you to think of here, and your Temba, and your new house with all your trees and your miles and miles of hills and mountains all round you—it was somehow nice and cosy and safe. Kirkwall is so on the edge of everything.'

Their conversation was stopped by Temba's getting up. Rob proudly exhibited her udder, so large that it stuck out behind, almost touching the fall-line of her tail. He squatted down beside her and drew milk from each teat. Having done it several times in the last few days he was enough of an expert to rouse admiration in

Kirsty.

'Can I do that too?' she asked eagerly.

'You can *try*,' he said, stepping back.

She succeeded easily, but she messed her fingers thoroughly with the yellowish creamy milk.

'Oh, good,' he said in surprise, 'you couldn't have done that yesterday. She's awfully close to calving. Dad will have to come and look at her as soon as he gets home.'

'You said she'd calve in June and this is the fourth of July.'

'I know, but she's overdue. They often are with their first calf.'

Kirsty wiped her fingers clean by running them through the long soft white hair of Temba's belly. Rob frowned, then reached for the fly-spray gun and used it on the place where she had wiped.

'Oh, sorry,' she said. 'You do fuss over her, don't you.'

They heard Rob's mother's voice calling from the house and realised it must be dinner-time. Meal-times had gone haywire that day because they had had a late breakfast in Aberdeen after meeting Kirsty off the ship from the Orkneys. She had come alone, starting on the very day that her school closed for the summer holidays.

'I'll race you to the garden gate,' challenged Rob, and they were off so quickly that Temba's head turned only in time to see the second pair of legs disappearing through the doorway. She stood staring after them in astonishment. What could be wrong with them, to make them fly like that on such a hot lazy day? She herself felt strangely reluctant to move at all. All she wanted was to lie down again and doze off into a dream that came to her so often nowadays—a dream about having a black shadow always beside her.

'Now I hope you're going to be sensible, Rob, and not keep poor Kirsty cooped up in that stuffy little shed all this lovely summer afternoon. You haven't even shown her the garden properly yet.'

'Oh, that's all right, Mum. If Temba hasn't started we're going into the forest. But we *must* go back at once and see—and then we *must* keep having a look at her every half hour.'

They found her lying down once more. It was hot in the shed and flies were buzzing, even more loudly than the drone of bees in the elder bushes outside. Rob used the spray-gun, then stood looking into her eyes. Sunshine poured in through doorway and window. Woodpigeons cooed in the fir forest. A cock's long-drawn-out crowing came drifting from a distant farm. Time was drowsing lazily through the long midsummer day.

'If you look close you can see yourself in her eyes,' he said. 'Come here, where I am.' He moved away and Kirsty took his place.

'Yes,' she said, 'and I do look small.'

'She's not cudding,' said Rob, 'and she's not sleepy. She may be having pains, so it's hopeful.'

They climbed through the fence into the fir wood and walked in silence on the deep soft carpet of rotted needles. The coolness and the smell were delicious. Soon they could see nothing but trees in every direction.

Kirsty stopped and looked about uneasily.

'How do you know which way to go back?'

'I just guess, usually. Dad used to come with me until I got the feel of it.'

'What do you do if you're lost?'

'You can't get lost in a hundred acre forest, not unless you walk in circles and you won't do that because the trees are planted in straight lines—follow a line and you're bound to come out.'

They came to a clearing where some trees had been felled. She sat down on a stump, studied the sky first through the feathery fir-tops, then turned gravely to him. 'I'd like to do a picture—of a little cottage in a forest like this, with its door open and a cat sleeping just inside—and smoke going up straight from its chimney. We don't have any forests in Orkney.'

'You're scared, aren't you?'

'Well, I would be if I was alone. But then I wouldn't ever *come*, alone.'

'I do, quite often.'

'What, get scared or come alone?'

'Both, as a matter of fact. You see more when you're scared.'

'It's funny,' she said, 'you're younger than I am and yet I always feel safe with you. You're rather brave, I suppose.'

He tossed his head and grinned. 'No, I'm just reliable. But my parents are worried about me.'

'Why are they?'

'I haven't made any friends at school—not real ones —and I think about God and things like that. And I'd

129

still like to read that Bible if I could.'

'What do you think God *is*, really, Rob?'

Frowning, he brought out a pocket knife and began cutting a switch off the trunk of the nearest tree. 'Well —one thing—he's there when anything's getting born —or dying—when it's all scary and you can't possibly *ever* be bored.'

'Oh, yes,' she said as if seeing light, 'that's one thing that really scares you, doesn't it, getting bored.'

He looked at his watch. 'Half an hour gone. Let's go.'

Temba was out in the field and she had developed.

'Oh, yes,' Rob said, 'there's definitely something happening. Look how she's moving the root of her tail. Oh, yes, and look at her shaking her head. That means pain. It's coming, Kirsty! Oh, isn't it ter-*rifi*-cally exciting!'

But the time dragged on. Temba lay down, she got up, she made water, she ground her teeth, she lay down again, she got up, she went back into the shed for a drink, she came out again, she lay down again. Rob could read in Kirsty's face that she was beginning to get fed-up.

'Dad will soon be here now,' he said. 'Let's go in the garden for a while.'

When his father arrived home he was taken to see Temba before being allowed in the house. He said she might be two hours, she might be six, but her udder was getting uncomfortably full. He would come out later on and see if she would yield any milk.

So the waiting had to go on until after tea, and then

until after Rob's father had fetched a bucket and sat down on Rob's stool beside Temba in the shed and drawn as much milk from her as he could get. She made no objection, but half a gallon was all she would give.

'The best thing now, Rob,' said his father when that was done, giving Temba another close inspection, 'is for you and Kirsty to go away and leave her completely alone for a couple of hours. She may be glad of a bit of privacy. There may be things going on in that mind of hers that we've no idea of. Give her some extra straw and then shut her in, then if she hasn't calved before dark it'll be easier to keep an eye on her.'

17
The Moment that
Punched a Hole in Time

It was about sunset-time when they left the garden again. Half way across the field they had to stop to listen, for strange sounds were reaching them from the shed, which had to be interpreted. Rob only needed three seconds, then he was away again as if at the crack of a starting pistol, leaving Kirsty yards behind.

While he was sliding back the bolt to open the door, she reached the open window and pulled herself up to look through. They both saw the calf at the same moment. It was lying stretched out on its side, with its head up, being licked by Temba, who was at the same time talking to it down her nose. The sounds she was making would be very close to human ones, if the human were half way between sobbing and laughing.

Rob entered at once, but Kirsty stayed at the window. Temba lifted her head, brought her nose round and shoved it against his chest, making a louder and more normal moo as she did so and drooling slime on him, then returned to her work.

He squatted down by the calf and lifted its tail. This was so wet and slimy that it slipped out of his hand the first time, but he tried again and saw that it was a bull. It could hardly be more than a few minutes old.

He stayed squatting there, looking at the great dark

bulk of Temba's body towering above him, feeling a sudden little pang of sympathy for this calf which had just been pushed out of that really safe home it had lived in for so long. Then he turned to Kirsty's awed face, staring in with all the evening sky behind it, her ginger curls full of sunset lights. She was entranced but frightened. Her eyes were, for once, not slits with teasing sea-green fires in them, they were wide and solemn, wider and more solemn even than they had been in front of her picture in the Arts Centre.

He must bring her inside, of course. He wanted her there close to him and the calf, and surely that was what she wanted too, but just for a moment he felt he would like to go on looking at her.

Yes, just for a moment. But then, what a moment it was, what a moment for tasting to the full, for remembering and recording before it escaped for ever. Yes, because it was so seldom that you could pick out the special moments while they were still happening. Usually they were gone before you recognised them, or perhaps you just caught a glimpse of them streaking off into the blue like the bob-tail and hind legs of a rabbit.

But this moment really was the most special of all the ones like it that he had ever had. And it seemed to be lasting. Instead of fading out when Kirsty joined him, it went steadily on. She came up close and he told her the calf was a bull. She touched it on its nose, the only part of it that didn't look slimy, then smiled sideways at Rob and leaned against him with an arm over his shoulder.

'I never *quite* believed it happened like this,' she murmured.

133

Rob said, 'Hard luck on Rombold, isn't it, not being here to see it. When *I* have children I shall want to be there when they're born.'

'Oh, *yes*, so shall I,' said Kirsty, and a second later added—'but then—of course—' She began to laugh.

He said quickly, 'Yes, you silly twit, *you*'ll be there borning them!'

Her laugh grew and grew, became a runaway pouring giggle that picked him up too and carried him off. Their laughter so filled the shed that Temba had to stop licking her baby and give them a doubtful look. Rob managed to get control of himself, smoothed his hands over her neck in the way she loved.

'It's all right, Temba. Kirsty and me aren't laughing at you, we're just laughing, that's all.'

Only it wasn't all, not at all, and he knew it wasn't even as he said it. For they were not laughing for nothing—oh, no. They were laughing because—oh, because life was so *terrifically* good. It was keeping its promises. Temba had kept her promise to Rombold, so surely he, Rob, would be able to keep his promise to Temba, wouldn't he? To make sure that she would have a happy life and an easy death? Oh yes, he could see his way clear to that now.

Some special moments become so very intense that they punch a hole in time. This was one of those moments. Rob knew it was not only doing strange things to time but also important things to him and Kirsty, which he could not quite understand. Were they perhaps peeping through the hole into their grown-up world that awaited them?